AMBUSHED

A rifle boomed, and Longarm's flat-brimmed Stetson went sailing across the brush. He struck the ground and landed on a tarantula that had been trying to get out of his way. The hairy spider jumped straight up into his face, and Longarm's heart skipped a beat. But the insect bounced off his cheek, then disappeared into the brush.

More rifle shots clipped leaves and branches over their heads, and then they both heard the sound of racing hooves.

"Something went wrong," Longarm said. "I'm afraid that my new deputies have all been shot. We'd better get help to them quick."

When they reached their horses and mounted up, they rode hard after the thin dust cloud moving southwest. *Four to two. Maybe five to our two*, he thought as they galloped through the sage not even thinking about the old treasure map or its promise of gold. So far, all they had found was heat, dust, and death.

—◆— **TABOR EVANS** ◆—

LONGARM

AND THE
KISSIN' COUSINS

J
JOVE BOOKS, NEW YORK

This is a work of fiction. Names, characters, places, and incidents either
are the product of the author's imagination or are used fictitiously,
and any resemblance to actual persons, living or dead, business
establishments, events, or locales is entirely coincidental.

LONGARM AND THE KISSIN' COUSINS

A Jove Book / published by arrangement with
the author

PRINTING HISTORY
Jove edition / September 2003

Copyright © 2003 by Penguin Group (USA) Inc.

For information address: The Berkley Publishing Group,
a division of Penguin Group (USA) Inc.,
375 Hudson Street, New York, New York 10014.

ISBN: 0-515-13599-2

A JOVE BOOK®
Jove Books are published by The Berkley Publishing Group,
a division of Penguin Group (USA) Inc.,
375 Hudson Street, New York, New York 10014.
JOVE and the "J" design
are trademarks belonging to Penguin Group (USA) Inc.

PRINTED IN THE UNITED STATES OF AMERICA

10 9 8 7 6 5 4 3 2 1

Chapter 1

Deputy U.S. Marshal Custis Long was in his Denver rooms, and had just finished making love to Miss Olivia Atwood, a striking woman he had been seeing for the past two months. Her long brown hair was mussed, and she wore her usual sensuous pout on her pretty lips as she lit a cigarette and then held the match to Longarm's cigar. Her large and luscious breasts were uncovered, and he could see that they were wet with perspiration. The rooms were almost suffocating on this hot August afternoon, and the thought occurred to Longarm that he needed to go up into the Rockies, where the air was pine-scented and cool. But Olivia wouldn't like that, and neither would Longarm's boss, Billy Vail.

"How was it this time?" Olivia asked, blowing a ring of smoke at his ceiling. "And I want you to tell me the truth."

It was a loaded question because their lovemaking, while satisfactory, had somehow lacked its former passion. Longarm leaned back against the head of his bed and smiled. "Any man would kill to make love to you, Olivia."

"That's not what I asked."

1

"It was great."

Her eyebrows arched in question. "Oh? I thought it was a little . . . mechanical."

Longarm studied her face while trying to figure out how to respond to that unexpected remark. Finally, he said, "It's probably ninety-five degrees in here. It might even be a hundred. I think the heat takes something out of our bedroom pleasures."

Olivia shook her head. "It wasn't the heat."

"Then maybe we're tired. You're working long hours at your millinery store, and I'm putting in a lot of hours down at the Federal Building."

"No, it's not that we're tired," she stated. "It goes deeper."

Longarm tried to hide his growing annoyance. "Then what do *you* think is wrong?"

"I think that you've lost your appetite for me, Custis. I think that you are bored with me and . . ."

Tears started to fill her eyes, and Longarm felt a familiar stab of guilt. "Olivia," he said, "you know that I love you. It's just that I'm tired of the heat and I'm going crazy working behind a desk at the Federal Building."

"You're completely bored," she said accusingly. "Bored with your job, and you're especially bored with me. That's what's wrong with our lovemaking."

Longarm went over to his dresser and poured them both a couple of glasses of good whiskey aware that Olivia's eyes were fixed upon him every moment. When he returned to the bed and handed her a glass, he said, "Okay, I am bored . . . but not with you. I'm just getting sick of my job and the never-ending paperwork. I need to be sent out on an assignment in the field before I get stale."

"But you told me that you were tired of always being on the move and that your last assignment in the Nevada desert was the absolute worst ever. Why, you were almost scalped by Paiutes and murdered by those Mormon renegades. When you got back here, I hardly recognized you because you were so thin and drawn. Your boss is just trying to give you time to recuperate."

"Nevada was a rough assignment, all right," he agreed. "But it wasn't Mormons who tried to murder me; it was a bunch of crazy and fallen-away Southern Baptists. Besides, how was I supposed to know that they would get so upset when one of their young wives broke her marriage vows?"

Olivia's eyes widened. "Is *that* what happened? You seduced a married woman? Custis, you told me they got mad at you because you had to arrest one of them for horse stealing!"

"Yeah," he added quickly, "that's right. The trouble was all because of a stolen horse. He was a valuable animal because of his speed."

Olivia cried, "Custis, you promised to be true to me when we were apart! And now I learn that the reason you were nearly killed in Nevada is because of a married woman."

Longarm gulped down his whiskey and headed for seconds. "Look," he said, realizing he was getting deeper and deeper into trouble, "I need some fresh air. Let's get dressed and go out for something to eat. Maybe it'll be cooled down in here by the time we return and we can talk in a more calm and civil manner."

Olivia jumped off the bed and snatched her clothes from the back of a chair. She marched into his kitchen, and Longarm could hear her ranting and raving with indignation. He'd made a serious slip of the tongue, and he figured it was going to be a long Sunday afternoon. But at least, if they were in the company of others, Olivia wouldn't go into hysterics.

The seat of the problem, as Longarm saw it, was that this woman wanted him to marry her and then quit his job as a lawman and open a shop downtown. She wanted him to change his entire life, but that just wasn't going to happen. Longarm knew that he wasn't cut out to sell merchandise and wear a suit and tie. He'd go crazy locked in some shop fawning over customers.

Longarm loved women and did not like to hurt their feelings, but Olivia was crowding him, and so he was going to have to figure out some way to end their increasingly stormy relationship. The problem was that Olivia was kind, rather well off, and beautiful, not to mention that she was a passionate woman who loved to make love.

Yes, Longarm thought, he was going to miss Olivia, but it was about time to cut the cord and regain his necessary freedom.

I'll pay for this afternoon's meal and then I'll just have to tell Olivia that it's over between us when we return here.

Longarm sighed because he did not relish the idea of having a painful breakup with Olivia Atwood.

But it must be done. It will be hard on both of us, but it's the honorable thing to do. Olivia's heart will be broken for a while, but will heal. And besides, she is so good-looking that men will be busting down her door once they realize that she is free and eligible again.

Having made the decision to dump Olivia in the kindest way possible, Longarm felt better. Tomorrow he would go in to see his boss and tell him that he was ready to leave town on any assignment available. In fact, the first assignment available, unless it was in Nevada's wilderness. He'd seen enough of that high desert country to last him at least another year. Maybe Billy would have some difficult and challenging case up in the cool Colorado Rockies, or perhaps in Wyoming or Montana, both personal favorites, although New Mexico or northern Arizona would suit him just fine.

"Custis?"

He looked up just in time to see Olivia racing back into

the bedroom with outstretched arms. "Oh, Custis, I'm sorry and take back everything I said about our lovemaking being mechanical!"

She struck him so hard that they both fell on the bed. Olivia tore off her blouse and smothered him with her breasts. "Take me again, you big wild beast!" she screamed. "And this time, ravish me until I scream for mercy!"

Longarm was fighting for breath. Olivia was a large woman, probably five feet nine and 150 pounds. And when she got excited, she was a real tiger.

Her breasts were slick, and she had grabbed the back of his head and jammed his face between them. Normally, it would have been a pleasurable experience, but with the heat and the sweat, he wasn't sure about that right now.

Olivia's hand gripped his flaccid manhood, and she began to pump it like she was trying to raise water from a deep well.

"Olivia," he gasped, "what . . ."

"No talk," she said, "just action. If you really love me, then prove it right now."

"But we just did this a few minutes ago."

"You can do it again. Come on, honey, I want you *now*!"

Longarm wasn't in the habit of being unable to perform under even the worst of circumstances. He was legendary in his pursuit of women, and there had been many times when out in the wilderness under great personal hardship, he had been able to rise to the occasion and leave women of all shapes and sizes howling with animal pleasure.

"All right," he growled, rolling Olivia over and then kissing her lips and breasts until she was panting. "You want it rough, then that's the way you'll have it."

"Yes! That's exactly what I want. Ride me hard!"

Longarm drove his immense rod into Olivia as if it were a war lance. She locked her long, slender legs around his waist, and they went at it like sex-starved maniacs. They were sweating, heaving, and groaning, and the bed creaked and sagged as their bodies produced sucking sounds, until they finally soared into a state of frenzied ecstasy.

Longarm rolled off the woman sweating like a race-horse and noting that she was just as wet and wrung out. It took them both several minutes before they could catch their breath.

"Custis?" she said with a wicked and wanton twist to her lips.

"Yeah?"

"That was incredibly special. Nothing mechanical about that bout of lovemaking."

Even his bones felt empty. "You can say that again."

"Maybe we just needed to let our bodies work things out between us," Olivia said, looking as pleased as a cat lapping warm milk. "Maybe we talk too much."

What was this "we" stuff? Olivia always had talked enough for them both, but Longarm thought it best not to point out that obvious fact, so he said, "Could be."

She rolled over on her side and peered down at his glistening staff. "You're *still* long and hard."

He was surprised to see that she was right. "It appears that I might be stuck."

Olivia laughed. "What do you mean, 'stuck'?"

"I don't know," he said, grinning at his own silliness. "But maybe that part of me enjoyed what we just did together so much that it doesn't know that there isn't any steam left in my boiler."

"You mean your balls?"

"Yeah, that's exactly what I mean."

"What a magnificent specimen of manhood you are and how lucky I am to be the recipient of your seed. Do you know what I was thinking?"

"No."

"It struck me that we would produce extraordinary children. Don't you agree?"

His stubborn erection took a sudden dive, and Longarm jumped up from the bed. "Let's not be talking about children."

"But we would create exceptional physical specimens," she excitedly insisted. "Why, if we had girls, they'd be like me, and the boys would be like you, and . . ."

"Olivia," he said, sweating even harder than when they had been locked in their passionate embrace. "We need to get some fresh air and good food. Let's get dressed and go for a walk. I'm about to suffocate."

Her smile died and she looked away, trying to hide her disappointment. "You never want to talk about us in the future. I don't even think you want us to have a future together."

Longarm shook his head with exasperation. "Can't we just get some air? I swear, it's hotter in this bedroom than in the Nevada desert. Come on, Olivia! Let's get out of here for a while."

"All right," she said, avoiding his eyes.

They ate at the Colfax Café, located only two blocks from the Colorado State Capitol Building and Longarm's Federal Building. The food was excellent, and the wine they ordered was from California's best vineyards, but their conversation was strained and their mood subdued.

"It's over between us," Olivia blurted out loudly as they waited for the check. "I can tell."

"What are you talking about?"

"Don't try to fool me, Custis. I can read you like a book and I know you want to say good-bye."

"Only for as long as it takes to go on an interesting assignment," he told her. "Then I'll rush back to you."

"No. In your heart, you really want to say good-bye to

7

me forever, but you're too much the Southern gentleman to tell me that outright."

Olivia smiled bravely, then reached into her purse and laid one hundred dollars on the white linen tablecloth.

Longarm stared at the money. "What is that for?"

She raised her voice. "Dammit, Custis, it's for your exceptional stud services."

His cheeks burned, and Longarm was mortified to realize that all the other diners were watching and listening with great interest. "Olivia, quit it! I'm buying this meal and then we are going to go for a walk and . . ."

"No," she said, rising from her chair. "I have my pride and I know when something is over. And don't worry about me. James Wilson, Arthur Peterson, and Charles Montrose have *all* proposed marriage to me in the last month."

"They have?" Longarm wasn't sure he was hearing correctly.

"Yes. And to a man, they are wealthy, respectable, and successful. The only reason that I've held them off so far is that none of them could possibly be as well endowed as you are."

"Olivia!" he pleaded, eyes jumping around the room, which was now dead silent except for their embarrassing conversation. "Are you going crazy? Sit down and kindly lower your voice."

"No," she told him. "I'm quitting you right now. A woman can't live for just seven inches of a man, and that's all you've ever really given me. Just that wonderful seven inches hanging between your legs."

Longarm lowered his head with a groan.

"Good-bye, you magnificent stallion."

He didn't even look up. "Good-bye, Olivia."

"You'll never have another woman who can hump better than me."

"Oh, for crying out . . ."

"Aren't you even going to ask which one of my suitors I've decided to marry?"

"No."

"I'll marry Charles. He dangles only five inches to your seven, but he has a far larger heart."

Longarm raised his head. "I wish you and Charles Montrose the very best and a long future together."

Miss Olivia Atwood tossed her glossy mane of hair and raised her chin proudly. "Thank you for that," she said before hurrying away.

Longarm desperately needed a strong drink.

"Seven inches?" an obese woman with diamonds on her chubby fingers asked loud enough to be heard by everyone in the café's dining room. "My, oh, my!"

"Shhh!" the smallish man across the table for her hissed. "That's . . . that's physically impossible."

"Not really," the woman mused aloud, staring at Denver's handsomest and most famous lawman, until Longarm jumped up from the table and escaped to the sound of twitters and ribald laughter.

It was almost ten o'clock that night when Longarm, somewhat inebriated, returned to his rooms not sure whether he should be happy or sad. He was still shocked and embarrassed by what had transpired at the Colfax Café, and vowed he would not return there for many months.

And although he was relieved that he was now free to take up the chase for new conquests, he was also feeling a bit melancholy at having lost Miss Atwood to some pompous twit named Charles Montrose.

Oh, well, Longarm thought, *I suppose it has all turned out best for the both of us. She wanted a successful businessman for a husband, and I wanted to . . . to just remain a good lawman. And there is nothing wrong with being a federal marshal, except that the pay is pitiful and the working conditions dangerous and often desperate. How-*

ever, a man should always do what he does best and not measure himself against others who just happen to make five or ten times his salary. No, a man should be content with his lot and never be envious as long as he takes pride in his chosen profession.

He nodded his head and tried his key in the door of his rooms resolving to return to work in the morning and demand from Marshal Billy Vail to be sent out on assignment . . . any assignment.

Suddenly, Longarm saw a movement out of the corner of his eye, and he twisted around, hand instinctively reaching for the Colt Model T he wore on his left hip, butt turned forward.

But he had been drinking and was a tad slow. A massive fist struck him on the side of his jaw, and Longarm was slammed against his door, his legs buckling at the knees. He looked up and saw a pair of thugs and a man dressed in a business suit.

"Do you want me to knock his teeth out?" one of the thugs asked.

"No, just castrate him."

The thug was huge and menacing. "Sir, what did you say?"

"Castrate Marshal Long!"

The thug looked at his accomplice with dull bewilderment, then turned back to the well-dressed man in charge. "Sir, I'd rather slit his throat than do that."

"She said he had *seven inches,*" the gentleman replied, his voice bitter. "I'd want to make sure that he never gets to use them on my fiancée again."

Longarm had heard enough to put the pieces together. The man in the suit had to be none other than Mr. Charles Montrose, Olivia's fiancé . . . and that meant he was consumed with jealousy and revenge.

Longarm gulped as a pocketknife clicked open and he realized that things were about to go from bad to worse.

Chapter 2

"Drag his damned pants down to his knees and castrate him!" the well-dressed gentleman yelled, voice shaking with rage.

The man who had caught Longarm with a lucky punch turned to his friend, who extended the pocketknife saying, "The blade is dull but it'll saw 'em off."

"Then give me a hand."

Longarm took this all in while still in a slight daze from the punch he'd taken. But now, as the smaller of the pair bent to unbuckle Longarm's belt and pull down his pants, he was finally beginning to shake off the effects of the stunning punch.

"I'm a federal marshal," he told the pair of thugs. "If you try and do what you've just been ordered, I'll make sure you both spend the rest of your miserable lives rotting in a federal prison."

The larger of the pair turned to the well-dressed gentleman. "You didn't say he was a *lawman*."

"He's nothing but a rapist with a badge. Cut him!"

"I can't do that," the thug whined. "You want me to slit his throat? I can do that, but I won't castrate a man. I just can't stomach it."

Longarm said, "Smart decision. Now you and your friend clear out while you can."

The big man nodded. "I guess I will. No hard feelings, Marshal?"

"Yeah, there's hard feelings," Longarm answered, reaching up to see if his throbbing jaw would still open and shut. "But we'll meet up again sometime and I'll even things out between us."

"Let's go," the big man said, handing the dull pocket-knife back to his friend.

The man giving them orders was incensed. "If you leave you won't get paid! Not a damned cent!"

The two thugs exchanged glances, and then the smaller one said, "Let's get paid anyway."

"Yeah, let's."

It took less than a heartbeat for the thugs to knock the gentleman down and then relieve him of his wallet. For good measure, the smaller man kicked him in the ribs twice, and would have kicked him in the face if Longarm hadn't shouted that they'd done enough damage.

"Well, Charles," Longarm said when the thieves had vanished, "I guess we've both learned a hard lesson."

Charles Montrose was of average size and in his early forties. His hands were well manicured and his hair was freshly cut. But right now, he was in agony and writhing on the floor.

"How . . . how did you know my name?" he managed to gasp.

"It was pretty easy to figure that Olivia left me this evening and then rushed over to tell you we'd broken up and that I had been her lover."

"I could have stood that," Montrose whispered, his face pale and his voice strained. "But why did she have to tell me that other part!"

"About my seven inches?"

Montrose just managed to nod his head.

"I don't know," Longarm answered. "But it seems to me that a woman who would torment you with that kind of information might not be the one that you should marry."

Charles Montrose stared at Longarm, and they both sat up on the doorstep. Montrose said, "She was in hysterics when she came to me."

"Olivia is often in hysterics."

"But she's beautiful and exciting and . . . and I love her."

"Then," Longarm told the man, "you have my sincere condolences." He frowned. "Were you serious about paying those two to castrate me?"

"Absolutely," Montrose said. "No man should have seven inches. It makes the rest of us mortals feel as small and inconsequential as pygmies."

"Listen here," Longarm began. "My father gave me a bit of wisdom when I entered my teens. Do you know what he told me about this subject of what we have dangling between our legs?"

"No, and I'm not sure that I want to hear your father's wisdom. I'm really not that well hung myself, and I expect I'll not be able to measure up to a man of your proportions."

"Don't let it bother you," Longarm consoled. "You see, my father told me that size doesn't matter when it comes to pleasuring a woman."

"Easy for a human stallion to say."

"No, it's true. He told me time and time again that it's not how deep we fish, but how well we can wiggle our worm."

Charles Montrose, still in intense pain, studied Longarm for a beat, and then he coughed up a painful laugh. "Are you joking? Your old man told you that?"

"Yep."

Montrose shook his head. "If that's true, there's hope for us normal-sized men."

"Of course there is," Longarm assured him. "And I'll tell you something else if you promise not to get angry."

"I hurt too damn much to get angry."

"Then what you need to know is that Olivia likes it rough. She prefers to think of herself as a mare in heat and her man as a stallion."

"You can't be serious!"

"I *am* serious. She won't be hurt . . . so don't misunderstand. But Olivia can't find it in herself to respect a man who is always a gentle lover."

Charles Montrose shook his head in near disbelief. "Is this true?"

"It's true," Longarm swore, thinking he might even forgive this insanely jealous and well-heeled man. "Just act like an untamed mustang stallion and she'll melt like butter in your bed."

"Holy cow!" Montrose whispered, coming very much alive. "I had Miss Atwood pegged all wrong."

"Olivia is complicated, but she does want a man who is successful and a pillar of the community. One who wears a suit and tie like you are wearing every single day and who will give her the finest that Denver has to offer."

"I'm pretty damned wealthy, if the truth be known."

"Then you'll be a fine match for Olivia."

"But will she be true to me as a wife?" Montrose took a deep breath. "I love her, but I don't want to marry a woman who can never forget your seven inches."

"Forget that!" Longarm said sharply. "Be a man and be yourself. Let her know who is the boss and that you expect her to be a respectable wife and mother. Unless I'm very wrong, Olivia will toe up to that mark, and I'm betting she'll make you a fine match."

Charles Montrose nodded, and Longarm could see the gleam of hope in his eyes. "Say, Marshal, you're an all-right fella after all. And I'm sorry that I hired that pair to cut off your balls."

"Never mind." Longarm stuck out his hand. "Are we square with each other now?"

"Yes we are," Montrose said, struggling to his feet. "But I am sure in a lot of pain."

"Let me check those ribs." Longarm touched the man's ribs, and although Montrose grunted with pain during the quick examination, Longarm was sure that nothing was broken. "Have a doctor look at them, but I expect that you'll be fine after a few days."

"This is all my fault," Montrose admitted. "I'd buy you a drink or two to show how I hold no hard feelings, but those thugs stole my wallet."

"I've got whiskey in my rooms, so I'll pour you a strong drink."

Montrose looked at the front door, and then his eyes drifted up to the rooftop of the three-story structure. "I could buy this entire building tomorrow and give you free rent for the rest of your life without giving it a moment's thought as to the expense. Hell, I could hire you to be my bodyguard at double what you're making with the federal government."

"No, thanks," Longarm said. "I like the job I have now. Just put what happened between Olivia and myself out of your mind and try and be happy together."

"I will," Montrose vowed.

Longarm massaged his jaw again and opened the door. His ears were still ringing from the punch, and he knew that his jaw would be as sore as Montrose's ribs in the morning. But everything considered, it had worked out all right. He was free of crazy, hysterical Olivia and no one had gotten badly hurt.

In his past, insane jealousy or love gone sour had often resulted in far worse consequences.

•   •   •

Longarm was awakened late the next morning with a loud pounding on his door, and his first thought was that Olivia had returned . . . maybe even with a gun in her hand.

"Who is it?" he shouted, instantly regretting that because of the intense pain that shot through this swollen jaw.

"It's your cousins, Ruby and Nola Bugabee from West Virginia!"

"Who?"

"Your cousins from West-by-Gawd-Virginia!"

They shouted their names again, and Longarm's eyes flew wide open because, come to think of it, he did have two cousins whose last name was Bugabee. They were hill people, and if he remembered correctly, wilder than weasels. The Bugabees had lived a couple of mountain ranges away, and they had never been close to Longarm's family, but they were genuinely related.

"Hang on!" Longarm called, again forgetting about his aching jaw as he jumped out of bed and hurried to get dressed. "I'll be with you in a minute."

"You slow or something?" one of them called. "Don't get fixed all up just because of us. We're used to clutter and filth."

As Longarm pulled on his pants, he tried to remember about the Bugabees. He'd only visited them a few times in his youth, and he remembered that the head of the clan made moonshine and was a rabid ex-Confederate who had lost one leg and one arm at some terrible battle in West Virginia. He'd returned to his hill country homestead a bitter and angry man who then fathered so many unwashed children that even he had trouble keeping up with their identities.

Funny, but Longarm had even forgotten Old Man Bugabee's first name.

Longarm was still only half dressed when he flung the door open to confront the strangest pair of blondes he'd

16

seen in many a moon. They were both tall and handsome in a rugged, backwoods fashion that Longarm well remembered. Both were probably in their early twenties, and their appearance was almost comical, starting at the top with their battered wide-brimmed straw hats decorated with what looked like white and black speckled chicken feathers. Their faded gingham dresses were ten years out of style, and their shoes were the same old clodhoppers that Longarm remembered having to wear as a boy. And the Bugabee girls were wearing the same ugly and sagging wool stockings. Trying, he supposed, to look worldly, they had smudged their cheeks and lips with vivid red lipstick, and wore necklaces made out of what appeared to be the spines of rattlesnakes.

"Howdy!" the six-footer said, sticking out her calloused hand and shaking Longarm's paw as if they were fellow mule skinners. "My name is Ruby! This here is my little sister, Nola."

Ruby's grip would have done any man proud. She had a direct gaze and long eyelashes. Her sister was a few inches shorter, but cute and not quite so forward. Nola just smiled shyly and didn't offer Longarm her hand. She had brown flecks in her blue eyes and dimples in her flaming-red cheeks.

Ruby jabbed her younger sister with a sharp elbow, eliciting a grunt, and then said, "Well, say something to the man, Nola!"

"Howdy-doo," Nola managed to say, giving Longarm a wholesome grin that showed a big gap between her front upper teeth. "Pleased to meet you, Cousin Custis!"

"Nola is sweet but a little on the slow side," said Ruby.

The younger sister's cheeks turned even redder. "No I'm not! I can read, can't I?"

"You can read your name and not much more," Ruby said. "Nola, I can out-read you any day of the week including Sundays."

17

"Can not!"

"Can too!"

Longarm thought his cousins were going to get into a fistfight, so he threw up his hands and said, "Hold on here a minute. It doesn't matter who reads the best. What are you doing here and how did you find me?"

"Don't you know?" Ruby asked, her eyes widening with surprise. "I thought our cousin Boris told you we were coming with *the map*."

Longarm was totally confused. "Why don't you girls both come inside. I'll make us some strong coffee and you can straighten out the confusion."

He ushered them inside noting that they needed baths far worse than they needed coffee. But that was an uncharitable thought, and he chided himself for it. After all, the Bugabees were poor, uneducated, and backwoods folks like so many in the West Virginia hills he still recalled fondly. But why this pair had come to Denver, and to pay him a visit, was beyond Longarm's imagination.

"You girls just make yourselves at home," he said, going into his little kitchen to boil coffee and wash a few cups.

"You sure have a nice place here," Ruby said. "Sure is different from where we all came from back in the hills."

"You're right about that."

"Do you like livin' in such a big city?"

"I don't live here much of the time," Longarm replied. "I spend most of my time out on assignments. You were just fortunate to find me in town."

"Is that a fact," Ruby said, coming to stand in the doorway and watch him. "Well, I do recall you always did have restless ways about you. Now, I hear that you're a famous lawman."

"Not true. I'm just a poor deputy marshal."

Ruby turned and surveyed Longarm's rooms. By Charles Montrose's standards, it was a hovel. But by the standards of these two backwoods girls, it was a palace. That just reinforced Longarm's resolve not to get caught up in comparing himself to others. Everything was relative to what you were accustomed to, and there was no shame in having less than the next person.

"You ever get married?" Ruby asked.

"Nope."

"Why not?" Nola asked, squeezing into the doorway to stand beside her sister.

"Well, I'm on the road too much to be a family man."

"I'll bet," Ruby said, "you ain't no stranger to pretty women."

"Ruby!" her sister said. "That's not a nice thing to say."

"Well, I'm sorry about that, but this place reeks of women's perfume, and that thing on the floor didn't come off'a no man, I promise you that."

Longarm spun around and hurried into the front room to see one of Oliva's chemises laying on the floor just behind the couch. He hurried over and grabbed the undergarment, then stuffed it behind one of the couch cushions. "Don't know how that got here," he said, stomping back into the kitchen.

"Sure you don't, Cousin. Ain't none of our never mind anyways."

Longarm rushed the coffee, and when it was ready, he asked, "Do you girls like sugar or cream?"

"We'll both have both and lots of it," Ruby said. "It sure is good to see how well you've done out West, Cousin Custis. Yes, sir-ree, you've done the family proud."

"I've done all right, but not as well as some," he said modestly. "A marshal's pay isn't the best, but I'm not one to complain."

"Yes, sir," Ruby said again, "this place of yours is mighty fine. Do you own the *whole* building?"

"No. Just these rooms."

"Well," she said, "how would you like to own this whole damned building?"

Longarm had to chuckle. "You're the second one to make me that silly offer. But I'll tell you what I told Charles Montrose. I don't want to own the building because then I'd have to take care of it and it would give me all sorts of worries."

"Makes sense, I guess," Nola said, "but I'd admire to own it."

"Well," Longarm told her, "what makes you think I know anything about Boris or a map?"

The sisters exchanged quick glances before Ruby blurted out, "We have a treasure map. A real by-Gawd Confederate treasure map!"

He missed the coffee cup and spilled a spoonful of sugar on his counter. "What are you talking about?"

"Do you know about the Battle of Picacho Peak down in the heart of Arizona that took place between our Johnny Rebs and the Blue Coats under Captain Calloway?"

"I think I once heard of it."

"I hope you have, because that's where your Uncle Willard Bugabee was shot and wounded while fighting for our Confederate cause! He got back to West Virginia, but later died of his wounds. And just before he went to see the Lord, he told us about his treasure and gave us the map that shows how to find it in Arizona."

"What treasure?"

Ruby rolled her eyes as if that was the stupidest question she'd ever heard. "Why, all that gold that he and his fellow cavalrymen took back from the Apache Indians, of course."

"You're way ahead of me," Longarm said, filling his own cup and taking a seat because this looked like it was going to be a long and confusing conversation.

"We have a map . . . or at least part of poor Willard's map. I just don't understand why his son Boris didn't show up looking for your help. We all knew you were living in Denver, and he was told to come straightaway here to find you. None of the rest of us Bugabees except for Uncle Willard had ever traveled farther west than the Mississippi River, and now he's dead."

"Well, his son Boris never visited me. When did he leave the hills of West Virginia?"

"About six months ago," Nora replied, suddenly looking very worried. "Boris was to come here and live with you until we arrived, and then . . . then we'd all go together to Arizona and get the treasure."

Longarm shook his head. "This whole thing sounds to me like a big hoax. Why, I've heard of the Superstitions and the lost treasures left there by the Conquistadors. But it's my belief that the Spaniards found no cities of gold, and I can't believe that your Uncle Willard and his Confederate friends found anything valuable either."

"Well, he did, and he is your uncle too. He died a war hero, and his name is sacred back where we grew up." Ruby was upset and her eyes were flashing. "Custis Long, we came a long, long way to help Boris, and the family back in West Virginia voted to cut you in on the hidden treasure."

"They did?"

"Sure, but your attitude is beginning to gall me."

Nola dipped her chin in agreement. "We expected better of you, Cousin."

"I'm sorry about that," he said. "I didn't mean any disrespect for Cousin Boris or Uncle Willard, but I still find this whole story preposterous."

"What?"

"Hard to believe," Longarm amended, knowing that they didn't understand. "You need to understand that half the people out West have treasure maps. You can go to any state or territory from Colorado up to Oregon and California and there are hidden treasures said to be found and plenty of charlatans who draw them up and sell them on city street corners."

"That might be true of folks out here," Ruby conceded, "but we're still thinkin' that given how far we've traveled, you could at least read Uncle Willard's last, dying words on paper and look at our half of the map. After that, if you still think this is all a lie, then we'll just go to Arizona by ourselves and find the treasure."

"You said you only have half the map."

"We have the biggest and most important half," Nola told him. "And besides, we aim to find out what happened to your cousin Boris. Maybe . . ."

Her voice choked up, and Ruby finished. "Custis, do you remember the Haskill clan from up near Clear Creek?"

"I remember them," Longarm said, a frown appearing on his forehead. "As I recall, they were all mean and dishonest. When I was small, some of the bigger Haskill boys used to chase me down and beat me senseless. The first one I ever whipped was that bully Jude Haskill; after the fight, I thought his kinfolk were going to kill him for losing and then me for winning."

"That sounds about right," Ruby said, "and Jude was always one of the meanest of the lot. What we haven't told you yet is that the Haskill clan learned about Uncle Willard's treasure map and now they're also after the gold. And guess what."

"What?" Longarm asked, feeling himself being drawn into the mystery.

"Not two weeks after Boris left home, three of the Haskill men headed West and they were led by Jude."

Longarm sipped his coffee. "They could have just gone hunting or trading. They might never even have gotten as far west as the Ohio River."

"They got farther than that," Nola said.

"How do you know?"

"We been trackin' 'em." Ruby looked Longarm square in the eye and added, "Because we mean to try and kill all three of them Haskills."

Longarm blinked. "Why?"

"Because they'll kill poor Boris, of course! And they'll kill us too if they think you know anything about the Picacho Peak treasure."

"Let me see the letter and the map."

"Actually," Ruby hedged, "we left the letter at home, but we memorized it. Willard had it written up by the schoolteacher, Mr. Kitchen, and he swore that he'd keep it a secret until Uncle Willard said otherwise. So when Uncle Willard died, Mr. Kitchen handed the letter and the map over to us as he'd promised. Here's our half of the map. Boris memorized it and took the other half."

Longarm waited while Ruby turned her back and dug the map out from some secret hiding place under her dress.

"Here's our half of the map," she said, handing it to him.

Longarm placed his cup of coffee down and unfolded the paper. It was smudged and wrinkled, so he tried to smooth it out, and then he studied it carefully. "This shows Tucson and the Superstition Mountains, but it's been cut in half way up to where Phoenix ought to be located," he said.

"That's because your cousin Boris took the northern half of the Arizona Territory."

Longarm was disappointed. "It appears to me that this map is mostly of the Superstitions and a lot of Arizona's desert country down to Mexico and over to the Colorado River."

He placed his finger on the map. "What is this big X supposed to mean?"

"That's where the treasure is buried!" Ruby said, looking excited. "Uncle Willard said that in his letter that we memorized."

"He sure did," Nola told Longarm. "The letter said that it was buried not far from Picacho Peak."

"But there's no mention of distances," Longarm said pointedly. "I mean, we don't know if this X is right on the side of the peak or if it's miles away."

"Boris's part of the map has the distances," Nola explained. "And a whole lot more."

"Have you seen his half of the map?" Longarm asked.

"Why, of course. We're the ones who cut it in half. Custis, we can find the treasure if we can find Boris."

He handed the map back to them. "I don't know about this."

"If you'd known Uncle Willard, you'd know he wasn't a liar. Why, all of our kinfolk used to call him Honest Willard. Isn't that right, Nola?"

"I swear that it is," she said. "Honest Willard was said never to tell a lie in his whole life. He was a righteous man."

"Very righteous," Ruby agreed. "But he hated the Yankees until the day that he died."

"Amen to that!" Nola said with surprising passion. "I hate 'em too."

Longarm shook his head. "The war is over. A lot of us came to the West needing to put the past into the past and let our hatred go."

"Uncle Willard wouldn't, and the war finally killed him," Nola said, her lips tight with the pain of recollection. "The wound he got at Picacho Peak never healed. It just festered and festered in his guts until it finally killed him."

"That's right," Ruby added. "He died hard, and you could hear his screams echoing up and down the hollows. The poor man was in terrible pain when he drew that map, and our uncle swore he wouldn't rest in peace until the

24

treasure was found and put to good use. That's why we got to find it, Custis. Because you know the Haskill boys won't put it to any good use. No, sir! They'll use it in every evil way possible."

"What good use were you thinking of spending the treasure on?" Longarm asked.

"After we paid you . . . of course . . . we'd take the rest back to the hills and use it to build a schoolhouse and maybe to fix up some of the people's houses. You remember how bad us folks live. Especially the old people that can't afford to fix their roofs or even a wood floor."

I remember," Longarm said. "And I recall that your schoolhouse was just a drafty little shack with a dirt floor."

"That's right. It's freezing cold in the winter and the roof leaks."

Nola placed a hand on Longarm's shoulder. "We sure could use your help in finding Boris. We're fearful that the Haskill men might already have found and killed him."

"Maybe even tortured him for what he memorized from Honest Willard's letter," Nola added. "We got to try and find him and maybe save his life, Custis. Won't you *please* help us?"

Longarm came to his feet and paced back and forth trying to decide what to do. As a veteran lawman, he was inclined to dismiss this whole story as utter nonsense. But he had seen half of the map, and he did recall that Uncle Willard Bugabee had been called Honest Willard. And what if his cousin Boris, who he remembered as a good lad, had been followed and either killed or taken hostage for his half of the map by Jude Haskill and his murdering brothers?

"Here's what I'll do," Longarm decide out loud. "We'll spend the day trying to find out if anyone in Denver has seen Boris Bugabee."

The two sisters jumped up into the air and hugged him until Longarm was half choked. "All right," he said, trying to calm them down. "Is our cousin still about five feet six inches tall and skinny?"

"Goodness, no!" Ruby said. "Boris is almost your size. He'd be nearly thirty years old."

"Twenty-nine," Nola corrected.

"Thirty."

"Twenty-nine!" Nola insisted, jaw clenched with stubbornness.

The sisters started wrangling again, so Longarm put a stop to that by saying, "You girls need to clean up and get some new things to wear."

"Why?" Nola asked.

"You just ought to have proper dresses and shoes," Longarm said, not wanting to hurt their feelings, but knowing full well that they stuck out like sore thumbs.

"We're a little on the light when it comes to funds," Ruby told him.

"I'm buying."

"Oh, we couldn't do that!" Nola exclaimed. "It wouldn't be proper."

But Longarm was insistent because he didn't want people to be staring at his West Virginia hill country cousins as if they were freaks or oddities. Ruby and Nola might be backwoods, but they were good and decent girls who obviously had courage or they would never have come looking for Boris and the treasure of Picacho Peak.

"Have you had any breakfast?" he asked.

They shook their heads.

"All right then," Longarm said. "While you bathe, I'll cook us breakfast."

"You can cook?" Nola said, looking stunned.

"When I have to. And after you've bathed and eaten, we'll go shopping, and then take up the hunt for Boris. Agreed?"

26

They exchanged glances, then nodded in unison.

"Good. Now let's get moving."

As Longarm fixed his cousins' breakfast, he weighed what he had just learned. He expected that . . . if Boris had even gotten as far as Denver . . . he might very well have gotten drunk, mugged, or thrown in the local jail. On the other hand, he might have lost confidence in the Arizona treasure and just taken a job or left town to vanish in the West. And finally, he might actually have been killed by Jude Haskill and his brothers. It was this last unlikely but possible outcome that convinced Longarm he had no choice but to do his best to find Boris Bugabee.

I have to go through the motions looking for him before I can convince those girls to give up on this wild-goose chase and go back home where they belong, Longarm thought. *And besides, I didn't much want to go to the office today anyway.*

Decision made, Longarm immediately felt better. He liked the Bugabee sisters, and he wanted to make damn sure that his two naïve cousins didn't get swallowed up in this big and dangerous city.

Chapter 3

"So where do we start looking for Boris?" Nola asked as they walked down West Colfax Avenue.

"After we get you some new clothes, we'll start at the city marshal's office. His name is Ben Leland and he's a good friend of mine. We've worked together plenty of times to catch thieves and murderers. If he or any of his deputies have seen Boris, then we can at least assume he got this far."

"Oh, I'm sure that he did," Nola said. "And he was going to look you up right away."

"Well," Longarm told her, "he didn't."

"What is that beautiful gold-crowned building?" Ruby asked.

"It's our state capitol," Longarm told her.

"Golly," Nola said, "don't you Coloradoans have anything better to do with your gold than to put it on the roof?"

Longarm smiled. "It's not solid gold. If it were, the roof would collapse under the huge weight. I think it's just a thin layer."

"Something that big and shiny ought to draw a lot of bird shit."

"I expect that it does, but I've never given it much thought," Longarm said, deciding to change the subject because of all the stares the oddly dressed Bugabee sisters were receiving.

He guided them into a women's dress shop that he knew would not be too expensive and said to the owner, a nice matronly woman named Beatrice, "These are my West Virginia cousins and I'd like you to fit 'em out with a couple of new outfits."

Beatrice raised her eyebrows. "Well," she said, "this will create quite the challenge because they are both rather tall and broad in the shoulders."

"We're *real* strong," Ruby said, displaying calluses on her hands. "And we didn't think there was anything wrong with our clothes, but Cousin Custis seems to think otherwise."

"We might start with your shoes," Beatrice said, unable to hide her distaste for the ugly clodhoppers, "and those . . . what are those necklaces made of?"

"Timber rattlers from back East. We killed 'em, skinned 'em, then boiled the bones. Pretty as pearls, ain't they!"

Beatrice's eyes widened, but otherwise, she hid her shock well. "They are quite . . . unusual, that's for sure. However, I think I have a few lovely but inexpensive beaded necklaces that would actually complement your graceful necks."

Nola encircled her neck with both of her large hands, looking like she was going to throttle herself. "You really think we have pretty necks?"

"Of course you do! Now let me show you these necklaces and we'll start trying on dresses and shoes for size." Beatrice looked at Longarm and said, "This is going to take all morning, and I'm sure that you don't want to wait around. Why don't you come back around noon. I hope you'll be pleasantly surprised."

In a low voice, Longarm whispered, "Do them proud, but try to keep the charge at fifty dollars."

"Not a chance," Beatrice whispered back as she hurried away.

Ruby came to Longarm. "This is real exciting, but I think we ought to try and find Cousin Boris before we get fancy clothes. I'm worried to death about that man."

"Look," Longarm replied, "while you're getting new clothes and shoes, I'll check in at my office to tell my boss what I'm up to today, and then maybe ask around about Boris."

"Can't we come with you and buy these things later?" Nola asked. "We'd enjoy a tour of the town while we're looking for Boris."

"We'll do that some other time," Longarm said, not at all wanting to have the people in his Federal Building see this pair dressed as they were right now. If that happened, he'd be teased at the office unmercifully for weeks. No, far better to get these backwoods girls gussied up first and then show them Denver. "Don't leave here until I get back."

"I'll watch over them," Beatrice promised. "Just don't get lost!"

Longarm understood her concern, and it occurred to him that the dress shop owner would more than earn her money this Monday morning.

"A bit late this morning, aren't we?" Marshal Billy Vail asked from behind his desk. "What's the matter, another rough night with the ladies? And isn't your jaw a bit swollen and discolored?"

"I got punched without warning last night," Longarm said. "But that's not what I want to talk about. Billy, I need some time off."

Billy never liked to give his deputies time off, preferring to keep them at his beck and call for unexpected emergencies. "How much time?"

"I don't know. Couple of days. Maybe just today." Longarm then went on to explain about the unexpected appearance of his two West Virginia cousins and the mystery of Boris and Honest Willard and the Picacho Peak gold.

The telling took a good fifteen minutes and all the while, Billy Vail did not interrupt once. He just leaned back in his office chair, steepled his stubby fingers, and listened like a father might listen to his troubled son.

"So that's it," Longarm said when the story was finished. "I hope you can understand why I have to help Nola and Ruby find Boris Bugabee."

"This whole story is pretty ludicrous," Billy said at last. "And I'm surprised that you would even get involved in such a farcical undertaking."

"They say that they've tracked Cousin Boris and the Haskill brothers, who I know are a bunch of cutthroats. Furthermore, I saw half of the Arizona treasure map, and recall that Willard was always called *Honest* Willard. So, if my distant uncle said that there was a fight between the Confederacy and the Union clear out in Arizona, I have to believe it to be fact and not fiction."

"Oh," Billy said, "there definitely was such a battle down in the hot, low scrub country of central Arizona. I have even visited the site."

"You have?"

"Certainly. I was once sent out on assignments, and you know that I've always been interested in history."

"That's right," Longarm said, looking at Billy's office walls plastered with maps and mementos of his exciting days when he was often in the saddle or on a murder case somewhere out in the Wild West.

"I remember very well," Billy continued, leaning even farther back in his chair and kicking his heels up on his desk, "that when I visited Picacho Peak, I retraced that historic battle, which, actually, was more of a skirmish. Both sides suffered only a few casualties, then beat a hasty retreat. The Confederates, who were mostly Texans, headed for Tucson, and were ordered to abandon the Arizona Territory and never return. It was estimated that only a few hundred rounds were fired in the battle, and that only four or five men died and no more than that number were wounded or captured."

"I'm surprised that you know Picacho Peak since what happened there wasn't important."

"It was *historically* important," Billy reminded him, "because it was the westernmost engagement of the entire Civil War. But it had no military or political impact, and so the battle is just a recent footnote on the pages of our colorful frontier history."

"I doubt that I'll even have to go there," Longarm said.

"I should hope not, but you might."

"I've got at least a month vacation time coming," Longarm said.

"It's August, and that's not the place you want to spend your vacation."

"I know. I was actually thinking of going up into the Rockies and doing some trout fishing."

"You're no fisherman. What you'd do is attract a couple of young, loose women, and return to your job more exhausted and beat-up than you are now."

"No," Longarm insisted. "I'm done with women for a while."

"Oh?" Billy asked, barely able to hide his sarcasm. "And why would a man like you say a thing like that?"

"I broke up with Miss Atwood last night."

Billy groaned. "Custis, you big fool. Miss Atwood was the best marriage prospect you've hooked up with in years. My Gawd, man, she had tons of money and was both charming and beautiful."

"I can't deny that, but there were things about Olivia that weren't at all evident on the surface."

"Poppycock!" Billy cried. "I've been telling you for months that you need to marry that woman, and from the rumors I've heard, she was crazy to marry you."

"Olivia wanted me to turn in my badge and become a businessman. Is that what you think I should be?"

Billy was rarely caught off guard, but this was one of those times, and he cleared his throat. "Of course not. You have no concept of business or bookkeeping. You'd give merchandise away to every hard-luck person who walked in your door, and you'd spend your profits on foolishness. Any business you started would quickly go bankrupt."

"Thanks for the compliments," Longarm said dryly. "So maybe it was just as well that me and Miss Atwood parted after all."

"Perhaps," Billy conceded. "At any rate, it sounds like those female cousins of yours are real hicks. Best thing you can do is watch out for them a few days, then get them back to the hills of West Virginia where they belong."

"They're insisting that they will push on to Arizona with or without me. They mean to find that treasure and use the money to help the poor hill country folks back home."

"If they found a real treasure of gold, do you actually think they'd give it over to charity?"

"If they weren't killed or robbed, I'm absolutely sure they would. Ruby and Nola are good girls."

"Well, they won't be if they hang around you for very long. Are they good-looking?"

"I'm not sure," Longarm said, explaining how he'd taken them down to be done over by a dress shop owner he knew and trusted. "I'm hoping she will turn them into becoming quite attractive young women."

"Women you will no doubt defrock and defile."

Longarm shook his head and his voice hardened. "Billy, these are cousins of mine."

"Distant cousins," Billy said. "More importantly, they are young women. If I were their father, I wouldn't trust you around them for a minute."

"Thanks for being so insulting," Longarm told the man. "The truth is they couldn't be in safer hands."

"Ha!"

Longarm was starting to do a slow steam. "What about the days off that I've requested?"

"All right,' Billy said. "Take the next day or two off, and if you need more time, then come in and we'll talk it over."

"Good enough."

Longarm was about to leave when Billy said, "Miss Atwood isn't going to change her mind about leaving you, is she? I mean, is it really over between you and her?"

"Our love is as dead as a doornail. Why are you asking?"

Billy dropped his feet to the floor and looked a little sheepish. "I've got a friend who would love to get to know Miss Atwood much better. He's long worshiped her from afar."

"Tell your friend to worship someone else in bed," Longarm said, "Mr. Charles Montrose is madly in love with Olivia, and she's decided to marry the man."

"Charles Montrose!" Billy exclaimed. "He's one of the wealthiest men in Denver and quite the sought-after bachelor."

"So he told me," Longarm said, walking out the door with no intention of telling his boss that Montrose had nearly got him castrated.

When he entered Beatrice's dress shop and saw his cousins, Longarm's jaw dropped almost to his knees.

"Like it?" Beatrice asked, hurrying over to take his arm and lead him forward.

Longarm couldn't take his eyes off his cousins. "They look . . . terrific!"

Nola and Ruby rushed over and gave Longarm a little bow that he guessed was supposed to be a curtsy.

"What do you really think?" Ruby gushed.

"I think you're both beautiful."

And that was the truth because Beatrice had worked magic on the pair, who now seemed like entirely different women. They each wore new dresses and beautiful beaded necklaces. They had been fitted with white shoes, and their new pink straw hats were feathered and stylish enough to gain them entry into any of Denver's finest establishments. Beatrice, bless her heart, had even talked the West Virginia sisters into getting rid of the garish red lipstick and rouge and replacing it with a much more subtle and flattering shade of pink.

"Why, you ladies are as pretty as princesses," Longarm said, doffing his snuff-brown hat and returning their bow. "If I didn't know it for sure, I'd swear that you were a couple of society girls from Boston."

Nola and Ruby blushed and actually tittered like a couple of schoolgirls. They were doing just fine until they each gave him a hug that would have done a grizzly proud.

After seeing his boss, Longarm had made a stop at his bank and had withdrawn a hundred dollars. "Beatrice," he said, "how much money do I owe you for doing such a fine job of outfitting my cousins?"

"Fifty dollars will do it. They've got extra outfits, which I'll have a seamstress work on this afternoon. It wasn't easy to find dresses that fit, but we did it. These two are going to draw men like bees to honey, so you had better watch out for them."

"We can handle ourselves when it comes to the men,"

Nola said, showing her fists. "Ruby and I know how to kick, gouge, bite, rip, and punch when we get cornered."

Beatrice was shocked, but managed to say, "Yes, I can believe that."

Longarm chuckled, and turned the subject back to money. "Beatrice," he began, "fifty dollars seems a bit on the light side considering the amazing transformation that you've accomplished with my cousins."

"You can pay me back the extra some other time and in some other way." Beatrice winked, and if Longarm hadn't known that the woman was happily married, he would have been taken aback by her remark.

Nola and Ruby thanked the dress shop owner profusely for her help and advice on how to use makeup and how to dress in the city. When they stepped out on the boardwalk, people were still staring just as they had earlier, but now the Bugabee girls were so well dressed and made up that the looks were of admiration rather than amusement.

"Where are we going first?" Ruby asked.

"To the city marshal's office," Longarm told her. "If Boris has been in town, most likely Marshal Leland has seen or heard of him."

"He stands out," Ruby said. "And there aren't many around here riding Missouri mules."

"He's riding a mule?" Longarm asked.

"Biggest, blackest mule you've ever laid eyes upon," Nola told him. "And it's stronger than an ox. Why, Boris has won plenty of money with that mule in pulling contests."

"Glad to hear that," Longarm said as they neared the marshal's office.

When they entered, Ben Leland was at his desk, and so were two of his longtime deputies, Joe and Monty, who knew and admired Longarm.

After the introductions and a brief explanation of why Ruby and Nola had come to Denver, Marshal Leland said,

"So you think your cousin Boris has been hurt or killed?"

"Yes, sir," Ruby replied. "Otherwise, he'd have found Custis and we'd all be together and gettin' ready to go to Arizona."

"For the treasure."

"That's right, Marshal."

Leland glanced at Longarm. "The man could have just ridden out of town or took a job or anything."

"That's what I tried to tell them, but they're sure Boris Bugabee made it at least this far."

"Fair enough, ladies. We'll sit down and you'll give me and my deputies a full description of your missing cousin."

When everyone was seated and the description had been given, the marshal said, "Boris sounds like a man that would be noticed and remembered. Straw hat, riding a mule, rail-thin, but very tall. Anything else you can add?"

"He had a black mustache and beard and wore a bowie knife on his left hip and a gun on his right. He had a Hawken rifle, and his mule had a big white patch on its shoulder where it had been bit when it was young and the hair growed in different."

The marshal was writing all of this down carefully, and said, "Anything else?"

"Not that that I can think of," Ruby said. "Other than his eyes were blue and he had a big half-moon-shaped scar way down low on his back."

"How'd you know that!" Nola demanded.

Ruby blushed. "I just remembered from when we was kids."

"He didn't get that scar until he was eighteen. And besides," the younger sister said, "it was on his . . ."

Longarm saw Nola's hand reach up to cover her mouth. "Where was that half-moon scar?" he asked. "It's important for us to know if we find a body."

"It was lower," Nola whispered, her cheeks now a deep crimson. "Down on his right cheek."

Ruby's eyes widened with shock. "Why you cheatin' little hussy! How'd *you* know!"

"Never mind!" Longarm said, just as Ruby was about to attack her sister in the marshal's office. "How Nola learned of Boris's scar just isn't that important right now."

"It is to me!" Ruby snapped. "Jezebel!"

Nola took a swing at Ruby but missed. Longarm and the marshal had to jump between them to head off a fight.

"Listen here," Longarm said, "we've no time for this nonsense. We need to start hunting for Boris, and we probably ought to begin at the three mortuaries in town."

The sisters's eyes widened and they forgot all about whipping each other. Ruby blurted out, "I sure hope we don't find poor Boris there."

"So do I," Longarm told her.

Marshal Leland said, "Do you want me to come with you?"

"No," Longarm decided. "If Boris has been murdered, we'll get back here soon enough and ask for your help."

"We'll be glad to give it, but maybe the man just gave up the treasure hunt and was offered a good job. It happens all the time."

"Maybe," Longarm said as he ushered his cousins out the door.

They started with the largest mortuary, and were relieved to learn that no body fitting Boris's description had been received.

"He's all right," Nola said. "Boris is skinny, but he's a bad man to tangle with in a fight. He can take care of himself."

Ruby wasn't so sure. "If Jude Haskill and his brothers got the jump on Boris, he'd have no chance at all."

Longarm kept his silence as they entered the second

mortuary, which was called the Heavenly Rest Mortuary. They were greeted by a short, bald man in his fifties who was surprisingly jolly given the nature of his profession.

"Describe your cousin," the undertaker said. "If we've handled him, I'll remember."

Ruby and Nola both described Boris, and the mortician nodded his head and said, "I'm afraid we might have him on ice right now."

"Oh, no!" Ruby cried.

"I'm sorry, but it does sound like the man you describe. Why don't we go into our heavenly ice garden and take a look."

Longarm thought that was an excellent idea, but he could see that both of the girls were suddenly deathly afraid of encountering a frozen Boris, so he said, "Wait here and I'll go have a look."

They seemed relieved.

"Right this way," the undertaker said cheerfully.

He led Custis down a hallway and into what had obviously been a walk-in bank vault. The "heavenly ice garden" had a massive steel door, and an attempt had been made to cover the outside combination lock with flowers. Inside, the walls were stacked from the floor to the ceiling with dripping blocks of ice, and the floor was two inches deep in water.

"You'll have to forgive us the water and conditions," the undertaker explained. "But in August . . . with this heat . . . it's not easy to keep the bodies frozen, much less chilled. And after a week, well, let's just say they get very ripe."

Longarm wasn't really listening as he sloshed over to the row of caskets, each draped with frosty blankets.

"Here," the undertaker said, drawing one of the blankets away and then slowly opening the plain wooden casket. "I didn't want to tell those ladies, but this man was found three nights ago horribly stabbed and beaten to

40

death. When you see the deceased's face and torso, I'm sure you'll agree that he was tortured. He was what we call a 'John Doe,' meaning that the deceased wore no identification nor did anyone appear to identify his body."

"Was the marshal's office notified?"

"Yes, but they sent over a new man who didn't want to enter this room. I insisted, but he got sick, and I heard later that he got drunk on the way back to his office and was immediately fired."

Longarm stared at the corpse and said, "Yes. This one does fit the description. But we need to turn him over."

"Why on earth would we do that?" the undertaker asked with dismay. "Don't you know that the blood pools on the lower half and . . ."

"I know that," Longarm said, no more eager than the undertaker to rotate the corpse in the tight confines of its casket. "But the man I am looking for has a prominent half-moon scar on his right buttocks."

"He will be slippery and difficult to maneuver."

"Let's each take one end. You take his head, I'll take his ankles, and let's twist like a big icicle."

The undertaker was getting upset, but he must have sensed that Longarm wasn't going to give up, so he did as he was told. The task did not go easy or well, and had the corpse been fat instead of rail-thin, they might have had to dump the body out of the crude casket and turn it over on the floor.

"It's him," Longarm declared, his expression grim as he stared at the large half-moon scar. "It's poor Boris Bugabee, all right."

"Then I'm sure that his cousins will want to see that he has a better casket than this one we use for paupers and 'John Does,' " the undertaker snapped, no longer pleasant.

"I don't know about that. Did you find anything on his person?"

"No. The man had been tortured and robbed. He had nothing but ragged clothing."

Longarm threw a hurried glance around the room, and he suddenly had a powerful urge to bolt and run. It wasn't that he hadn't seen more than his share of death; it was just that the surroundings were weird and he wanted to get away as quickly as possible.

"Let's get him turned around and get out of here fast," Longarm said.

"Good idea!"

They got poor Boris Bugabee onto his back, and Longarm forced himself to take a final look at his childhood acquaintance, a distant cousin. Boris's face was battered to a pulp, there were stab wounds on his arms and chest, and his throat had been cut from ear to ear. Whoever had done this had been demented.

Longarm shook his head. "Boris came all the way from the backwoods of West Virginia to Denver looking for me," Longarm said. "I wish he'd have found me before someone with murder in their heart found him."

"It is rare that we see this violent a death. Frankly, it bothered me greatly, and I've seen so much death that I rarely am shaken. But with this young man, I had nightmares."

"I understand," Longarm said. "I'm going to go see the marshal and make sure that he's aware of this. Then, we'll try to find out who did it."

"Good luck. This man was brought here by someone who left the corpse at our back door without a name or note. We, of course, had no choice but to take care of him even without the hope of being reimbursed. It's something we have to do out of a moral obligation to the dead."

"I appreciate that," Longarm said. "And I'll make sure that you are paid for your work."

"Thank you."

Longarm left the room, and his face was grim and set when he returned to the sisters and told them that, indeed, the corpse was none other than poor Boris.

Both girls burst into a torrent of tears, and Longarm held them close while they cried their hearts out.

"We'll find out who did this," he promised.

"It was Jude Haskill and his brothers," Ruby told him. "They tortured and then killed poor cousin Boris and then they kept his half of our map."

"I'm afraid that's probably true."

"And . . . and they've already gone to Arizona hoping to find the treasure," Nola said.

"Then that's where we're going!" he said.

They hugged Longarm and cried even more. Longarm gave them all the time that they needed. But as the minutes passed, his anger grew hotter and his need to kill Jude Haskill and his murdering brothers became an obsession.

Chapter 4

Longarm left the Bugabee girls at a women's boarding-house promising to see them at supper time, and hurried on to visit Marshal Ben Leland. When Longarm told him about the corpse in the mortuary, Leland was upset.

"I sent a brand-new deputy over there and he got drunk on the way back to the office. I was so angry that I never even thought to find out why the man got drunk and quit."

"We all make mistakes," Longarm said. "What I'd like you and your deputies to do is investigate and see if you can find out anything more about the murder before I leave town. There's not much to go on, and I'll also be asking questions and poking around."

"Does anyone even know where Bugabee was staying? Maybe he had some belongings and they're still stashed in a hotel room or boardinghouse."

"That's certainly a possibility," Longarm said. "If a couple of your deputies could cover those places, it would be a real help."

"We've got the deceased's description, but perhaps we ought to see him at the mortuary so that we can better—"

"I wouldn't recommend that," Longarm told the city marshal. "If it hadn't been for that scar on his right but-

45

tocks, I probably wouldn't have been able to make an identification. I hadn't seen Boris since we were kids, and he'd changed. But mostly, someone had really worked him over. I think he was tortured for his knowledge of the Picacho Peak treasure."

"Do you really believe it exists?"

"I don't know, but maybe that doesn't even matter anymore. I'd bet anything that Boris was murdered by the Haskills, and I'm going after them."

"To Arizona in August. I don't envy you that," Marshal Leland said, shaking his head. "It's going to be hot as hell unless you are going to the high country up north around Flagstaff or over on the Mogollon Rim."

"I wish I was," Longarm told him, "but Picacho Peak is right smack dab between Phoenix and Tucson, so it's in the low desert country."

"Damn shame. Well, Custis, let me see what we can find out before you leave. By the way, *when* are you leaving?"

"Tomorrow morning. I don't expect to get out of here early. I need to pack and make some preparations."

"Is the government paying for this trip?"

"Afraid not. This is family business even though it's been years since I've been home. Boris Bugabee was only a distant cousin, but you know the old saying about blood being thicker than water. And besides, if I don't go, those sisters will head for Arizona anyway, and I couldn't bear the thought of them getting the same treatment as that poor devil in the mortuary."

"Being women, they could even get worse," the marshal said, his meaning clear.

Longarm left the office and headed for the Federal Building to tell his boss of his plans. He was thinking that this trip would wipe out his savings, and that he needed to also pay the undertaker something for taking care of Boris. There went his plans for buying a new suit and shoes. Oh, well, now that he wasn't seeing Olivia anymore, he didn't need to worry about appearances.

He stopped at the bank and emptied out his account, then went to the Federal Building. Billy Vail was in a meeting, so Longarm had to wait nearly an hour before his boss appeared.

"You look upset," Billy said when he returned to his office with Longarm close on his heels. "Like you've seen a ghost."

"Worse than that," Longarm told him. "I just saw the corpse of a man who was badly tortured before he was murdered."

"A relative from West Virginia?"

"A distant cousin, but one that I had fond memories of."

"Tell me about it," Billy said, taking a seat and motioning Longarm to do the same.

Longarm quickly told Billy what he'd found, and ended by saying, "I'm heading for Arizona tomorrow. I'll catch the Denver and Rio Grande, then the Santa Fe."

"What about Ruby and Nola?"

"I doubt I could stop them with bullets."

"You could be getting yourself into a hell of a mess," Billy said with his typical bluntness. "And I just received word that we need to send a man to Cody, Wyoming."

"Cody sounds better than the Arizona desert at this time of year, but I can't do it," Longarm said. "I just emptied the last few dollars out of my savings account, and I am sure that I'll have to foot the bill for my cousins."

"Are you certain you want to do this?"

"I *have* to do it, Billy. Maybe, if I hadn't seen what was done to Boris, I could have talked myself into backing out, but not now."

"But you don't even know that your cousin was murdered over this silly treasure business! Why, he might simply have gotten mixed up with the wrong bunch."

47

"Not likely," Longarm argued. "The man was tortured. That tells me that it wasn't just a simple robbery and murder. Or a bad fight between a couple of drunks. No, whoever killed Boris tortured him for a reason, and since he owned nothing but the clothes on his back and maybe a few things stashed in some cheap hotel, it had to be about Picacho Peak."

Billy's expression grew troubled. "Listen," he finally offered, "you could do some government business for this agency down in Tucson, and that way your expenses would be fully covered."

"They would be?"

"Sure. There has been some trouble with the federal banking system down in Tucson. One bank in particular might be embezzling government funds and using the money for purposes that are not in this country's best interests."

"Be more specific."

"We're hearing rumors that there might be another revolution across our southern border. I'd like to find out if that bank is trying to finance something down in Mexico."

"You know that's not the kind of investigation where I do my best work."

"Yeah," Billy said, "but you could nose around and let us know if we need to send a federal bank examiner down there to really dig into things or not."

"I sure could do that much, and it would really help save me some money."

"Then it's done," Billy said. "I'll write out the paperwork and you can get some travel expense money this afternoon. Will three hundred dollars be enough?"

Longarm grinned. "You bet."

He knew what Billy Vail was doing for him, and it was greatly appreciated. If he cut corners, three hundred dollars would not only cover his expenses, but Ruby and

Nola's as well. He'd be frugal and so would the girls. "Thanks aplenty."

"Just make sure you do your job down in Tucson and telegraph me with a full report on what you think is going on with that bank. I have a feeling we need to plug some holes in the system before a dribble becomes a huge drain on our southwest federal banking system."

"I'll do it," Longarm promised.

"Watch out for those kissin' cousins of yours," Billy said with a sly smile.

"What do you mean?" Longarm asked, pausing at the door.

"I mean don't do too much kissin' or you could get your bare ass shot clean off."

Longarm shook his head. "For crying out loud, Boss. These gals are my cousins."

"*Distant* cousins, and if they are good-looking and willing, I doubt it would matter if they were your *sisters*."

Longarm didn't know if Billy Vail was serious or just pulling his cord to get a reaction, so he pretended to be hurt. "That's a hell of a thing to say about a man . . . one of your friends and best deputies."

"That could be true, but it's also true that you'll pork anything in a skirt."

"Damn," Longarm said, shaking his head as if the insult weighed heavy on his heart, "you're a hard, hard man."

"I just know you, Custis. And I want you to keep your guard and your pants up."

"So long, Billy. And don't let the dust and paperwork pile up too high while I'm gone."

Longarm bought the supplies he knew he'd need on the trip, and then he spent the rest of the afternoon going to the saloons and the livery stables. He was looking for someone who remembered Boris Bugabee, a man who would have stood out in Denver like ragweed in a rose garden.

He must have visited ten saloons before he got lucky. The regular bartender at the Spanish Bit Saloon said, "Yeah, I remember that fella. He was real thin and talked funny. He didn't have much money, but did have a pretty strong thirst."

"Was he alone?"

The bartender thought a moment and then said, "I believe he was. The thing that I remember was that he said he was going to find gold in Arizona. Of course, I've heard that kind of talk as long as I've been pouring drinks. But this fella, well, he got pretty drunk on our low-grade whiskey, and that's when he pulled out this tattered old map that he wanted to show around."

Longarm scowled. "I didn't recall Boris as being that stupid."

"I told the man to go get some sleep and stop spouting off at the mouth. No one was taking him or his treasure map seriously."

"Someone did, because he wound up dead."

The bartender's eyes widened with surprise. "Is that a fact?"

"Yeah. Boris was from West Virginia and one of my distant cousins. I'm trying to find out who tortured and murdered him."

The bartender sighed. "The man was a fool, but there was something about him that me and most of the others here liked. Your cousin didn't brag, and he looked so poor that quite a few of my customers bought him a round. He said he had this fine black mule that he was real proud of and was worth five hundred dollars. Can you imagine that! Five hundred dollars for a mule."

"Did he say where the mule was being boarded?"

The bartender thought about that for several moments, and then he replied, "I think he said the mule was being kept down at the Clinch Stables. You know, that run-down place out by Cherry Creek where the stagecoach used to stop?"

"I know it well," Longarm said. "Anything else you can remember? Maybe some of your other customers watching him very closely?"

"Sorry, but he seemed to be all by himself. That man sang us a couple of hill country songs to the accompaniment of our piano player, and he had a surprisingly good voice. Best I've heard in years. He was a fine tenor. I'm sorry to hear he was murdered."

"Me too," Longarm said. "I'd have liked to have gotten reacquainted with him after a lot of years. He came from good folks back in West Virginia."

"You're from the South?"

"That's right."

"Fought in the war on the side of the Johnny Rebs, did you, Marshal?"

"It's all history," Longarm said, pressed for time and anxious to see what could be learned at the Clinch Stables.

It took him less than half an hour to reach the stables and find the owner, a man as unkempt as his decrepit buildings and corrals. The stables had once had a sterling reputation and had attracted Denver's social elite. But over the years, they had fallen on hard times, and gone through half-a-dozen owners, who had all gone bankrupt because of poor management. Now, it looked to Longarm as if this owner was close to going under.

Longarm showed the man his badge, and learned that the new stable owner's name was Paul Dingman. "I'm investigating a murder," he said.

Dingman threw up his dirty hands. He was nearly toothless and had one eye that roamed. Longarm thought he was about as disreputable-looking a fellow as he'd seen in quite some time.

"Listen here, Marshal, I don't know nothing about a murder."

"I didn't say you did," Longarm told the man, "but you're boarding the deceased's black mule."

Dingman gulped. "Well, sir. I *was* boarding that mule, but three fellas came and told me that it was them that owned the mule."

"And so you just gave the mule to them without any proof of ownership?"

"Marshal, they was pretty hard-looking fellas, and talked like the one that had left the mule here, so . . . what was I supposed to do, fight all three?"

"I guess not. When did they collect the mule and what did they look like? I want a full and complete description."

Once Dingman saw that he wasn't going to be arrested for giving away the mule, he was more than eager to cooperate. "There were three of them and they all kind of looked alike. Big men with suspenders and heavy work boots. Black beards and long, tough faces. They were heavily armed and none too gentlemanly, I'll tell you for certain."

"What kind of horses were they riding?"

"They were riding mules."

"All three?"

"That's right. Big ugly mules just like the one they took. And they had pack animals, but they were sorry-looking horses."

"What color were the mules?"

"Just ordinary colors. Bays, I think."

"When they took the black mule, which way did they head?"

"South." Dingman pointed. "I was real glad to see them leave. I could tell they were men not to be trifled with. I had the feeling that they'd have gutted me without no more remorse than if they were stepping on an ant."

"You were right about that," Longarm said. "Is there anything more that they said you can remember?"

"Nope."

"When did they pick up the black mule?"

"Three days ago, or maybe four."

Longarm figured he'd gotten all the information he was going to get from Dingman, so he headed back downtown. It was nearly six o'clock, and he knew that the Bugabee sisters were waiting, no doubt anxious and hungry.

"Maybe the better way to do this is just to rent three horses and head out after them," he said to himself as he walked swiftly back to their boardinghouse. "I might get lucky and overtake Jude and his brothers before too many miles."

The more Longarm thought about that, the more it made sense. Three big men with four mules and a couple of packhorses would be remembered. With luck, Longarm figured he might be able to catch them before they got across the Rocky Mountains of Colorado.

It seemed worth a try.

"Custis!"

Longarm was just opening the picket fence gate of the boardinghouse when Ruby came flying off the porch. "Custis, my sister is missing!"

"What?"

"She's missing. Nola went out to get something for us to eat while we waited for you, and she never came back."

Longarm felt his pulse quicken. "Maybe she got lost. You and your sister aren't accustomed to cities. She probably got lost."

"Maybe," Ruby said, "but she was only going to that little market just up the street. Nola said she could buy us some apples to munch on while we waited. I can almost see the place from here, Custis."

"Have you been there asking for her?"

"Yes. They said she bought apples and then left."

"Did they say which way she turned when she stepped out of the market?"

"No," Ruby admitted, "and I didn't ask."

"Let's ask," Longarm told his cousin, taking her hand and almost pulling her toward the street.

"Oh, my heavens," Ruby said, "what if the Haskill brothers snatched poor Nola and cut her throat like they did to Boris!"

"Don't even think about it," Longarm snapped. "You still have the southern half of the treasure map, don't you."

"Yes," she said, patting her bosom.

"I'm sure your sister just got turned around and then lost. How long has she been gone?"

"Four hours."

Longarm groaned. Four hours was long enough for Nola to have gotten help, or even to have covered most of Denver on foot. Suddenly, things didn't look too good.

"Was your sister in the habit of taking long walks?" he asked hopefully.

"Nope. She said that she was afraid of so many people staring at us and that she'd be awfully glad to leave Denver. Nola wouldn't have just gone wandering. Not for love nor money would she have done anything but head back to our boardinghouse."

They practically ran to the market, and the proprietor didn't have any thing new to tell Longarm. When they left, Ruby said, "I am scared to death of what might have happened. What if Jude and his brothers got Nola and are doing to her what they did to poor Boris?"

Ruby's eyes were filled with tears, and Longarm could see that the woman was right on the edge of panic . . . and with good reason.

"Look," he said, trying to calm her worst fears. "I found out where Boris left his mule. The Haskill brothers came and took the mule, and I'm sure now that they killed Boris, got his mule and probably his half of the treasure map, and headed for Arizona."

"But what if they didn't?"

"Then they ought to be easy to find unless . . ."

"Unless what?"

"Unless one or two stayed here in Denver on orders from Jude to get hold of the other half of the map."

"But I have the other half of the treasure map, so they'd be coming after me next."

"That's right."

"We can't let them kill or torture Nola," Ruby said, changing the subject.

"I know that," Longarm said, "but Denver is a big, big city. It will be difficult if not impossible to find and save Nola, but we'll try."

"How?"

"We'll get the marshal and his deputies to help, and then we'll all just have to ask anyone and everyone we meet and cross our fingers that we get real lucky."

Ruby looked at all the thousands of people on the street and shook her head. "Custis, it appears to me that the odds of finding someone who has seen the Haskill boys snatch Nola is worse'n trying to find a needle in a haystack."

"It's all I can think of right now," Longarm told her as they hurried on toward the marshal's office. They were both out of breath when they burst inside the office.

"That's him!" Ruby screamed. "That's Ernie Haskill!"

Longarm barged across the room and grabbed the jail cell bars. "All right, Ernie, where is Nola!"

"Who the hell are you talkin' about?" Ernie drawled, not rising from the little straw mattress where he lay smoking a cigarette.

Longarm twisted around to face the town marshal. "Miss Nola Bugabee is missing, and we're pretty sure this man or one of his brothers grabbed her off the street this afternoon. We need to find her before she's tortured or murdered."

"Settle down," Denver's city marshal said. "We arrested this man because he was seen struggling with a woman. But she broke away and ran. We didn't know it was your cousin."

"Where did the woman go?" Ruby demanded.

The marshal shook his head. "We have a witness that claims the woman was screaming as she ran down an alley, but then she disappeared."

Longarm slammed his fist down hard on a desk. "This means that there were others involved; after Nola ran down the alley, they caught and took her somewhere by force. We've got no time to waste."

Longarm turned back to the cell and said to the smirking prisoner, "Where is Miss Bugabee?"

The big woodsman from West Virginia blew a smoke ring in the air. "I don't know what in the hell you are talking about, mister."

Longarm swung around and said, "Ben, this man is lying and a woman's life is in danger. We have to find out where they are staying and we have to do it right now."

Marshal Leland nodded. "I believe you, Custis, but what can we do?"

"Open the cell, Ben."

"Now wait a minute, Custis. What have you got in mind?"

"You don't want to know. Leave the office and don't come back until I tell you. Ruby, do the same. I'm going to have a very private talk with Ernie."

Hearing this made the prisoner sit up straight. "Now hold on there," he said, still puffing on his cigarette. "You can't just come in here and shoot me."

"Then you'd better sing like a bird," Longarm said between clenched teeth.

56

Ernie turned to Ben Leland, and now there was a tremble in his voice. "You can't let Custis Long hurt me. I'm under your damned protection now."

"He's right," Leland said to Longarm. "I can't let you harm a prisoner in custody."

"We're friends, aren't we?"

"Yes, but—"

"Then you'll have to take my word that there's no time to waste in finding out where this man's brothers or cousins or uncles have taken Nola. She'll be dead before morning . . . if she isn't already. Now do as I say, Ben. Just leave for a while."

"If you kill that man, I'll be charged as an accomplice for murder."

Longarm walked up to the marshal and said in a low voice that was meant to be shared by no one but his friend, "I won't kill your prisoner. You've my word on that."

"Or beat him half to death?"

Longarm drew the line at that point. "I'm going to do whatever it takes short of killing Ernie Haskill in order to save Nola's life."

Marshal Leland said, "I'm holding you at your word, Custis. Don't make me regret leaving you alone with my prisoner."

"A half hour ought to do it," Longarm said. "Take Ruby with you because this isn't going to be pretty."

"I'm staying," she said. "I know Ernie better than you and I can judge true if he's lying. Custis, there's no time to make a mistake, not if we want to save my poor sister."

Longarm knew the woman was right, and that she had a strong stomach. "All right," he agreed. "Everyone else leaves."

Ernie saw the way the wind was blowing, and he hurled the butt of his cigarette down on the floor of his cell and pleaded, "Marshal, you can't let Custis have his way with me! He'll *kill* me if you leave!"

To Ben Leland's credit, he just shrugged his broad shoulders, gathered his deputies, and headed for the door.

"Marshal, don't let him at me!" Ernie wailed.

But it was too late. Longarm was already grabbing the keys to his cell, and there was a smile on his lips that made Ernie's blood run cold.

Chapter 5

When the outer door slammed shut and his protectors were gone, Ernie Haskill put his back to the wall and clenched his fists. "If you kill me, you'll never find out what happened to her, and I ain't going to tell you nothin' anyway."

Longarm swung the cell door open and glared at the man he was about to punish. "I remember you from when I was a kid. You were Jude's youngest brother, and it's plain to see that you've turned out just as mean."

"My family never liked the Longs," Ernie hissed. "You thinkin' you were so high-and-mighty just because your pa had the best farmland."

"I've no interest in talking about the past," Longarm said, handing his six-gun to Ruby. "If you have to shoot him . . . do it."

Ruby cocked the weapon and asked, "What are you going to do to Ernie?"

Longarm ignored the question and turned to face the prisoner. In a voice made all the more ominous because it was soft, he asked, "Were you one of the men that tortured, then murdered our cousin?"

"I don't know nothing about Boris Bugabee."

Longarm took a step forward, clenching his own fists. "Sure you do. But before we talk about that, you're going to tell me where Jude and the rest took Nola. And you're going to tell it to me quick."

"No, I ain't!"

Longarm took a step forward, faked an overhand right, and instead threw a left uppercut that caught Ernie right below where his ribs met. It was a powerful and punishing blow that sent the prisoner to the floor gasping like a fish out of water. Longarm measured his next punch and caught Ernie on the cheek, crushing his orbital bones so that the man's eyeball almost popped loose.

"Please don't hit me no more!" Ernie cried, covering his already bloody face. "Please don't!"

In reply, Longarm grabbed the man by his dirty hair, bent his head back, and swore, "Next one crushes your windpipe. Do you know what that will do?"

Ernie's eyes were swimming in terror.

"When I crush your windpipe, your throat will tighten up around it and you won't be able to breathe and you'll drown in your own blood. There won't be anything I can do or even a doctor could do to save you as your throat slowly swells and cuts off your air. It'll be worse than a hanging, Ernie. A hanging is supposed to break your neck so you die quick. But *you* won't die quick."

Ernie became hysterical and started to beg as Longarm raised his big fist and took aim on the man's exposed throat.

"Custis, please!" Ruby cried. "If he dies so will my sister!"

Longarm lowered his fist and pulled Ernie's head back even harder. "You want to tell me where Nola and your friends are right now . . . or do you want to drown in choking agony?"

"I'll tell you!" the man screamed.

Longarm released his hair and let Ernie fall to the floor,

still quivering with pain and trying to hold his eyeball in place.

"Where are they?" Longarm demanded.

"In an old abandoned farmhouse just east of town."

"*Who* is in the farmhouse?"

"Clem, Bobby, Earl. And Nola Bugabee. That's all, I swear it!"

"What about Jude?" Longarm demanded.

"I don't know where he and the others went. Maybe on to Arizona. Yeah, I think they headed on to Arizona."

Longarm raised his fist, and Ernie cringed and howled, "I'm telling you the truth! Jude told us to get the other half of the map. We got one half from Boris, but the other half was missing and we figured it was with either Nola or Ruby. Nola was the first one we could grab."

Longarm yanked the man to his feet. Blood was gushing down his cheek from the shattered eye socket, and he was still trying to suck air. "We're going to get Nola right now," said Longarm.

"If I go with you, they'll know I told you and kill me for sure!"

"It seems you're damned if you do help me and damned if you don't. But if I were you, I'd rather take my chances going out to that farmhouse."

"If I take you there, will you set me free?"

"You'll stand trial for murder and kidnapping, just like the rest of them that survive."

"I'll take you there if you promise to give me a running start. I got to have some chance; otherwise you might as well kill me right now."

"Running start for where?"

"West Virginia! I want to go home."

"All right," Longarm finally agreed.

"That's all I ask. Just a chance, Custis. I never did you no harm when we were kids. It was Jude that hated you . . . not me. Just a chance is all I'm asking for."

"I'll give you the same chance you gave Boris and Nola," Longarm grated. "That's what you'll get . . . no less and no more."

Longarm hauled the man out of his cell, then found a washcloth and told him to hold it against his smashed cheekbones, then turned to Ruby. "Tell Marshal Leland that he and his men can come back now."

When the marshal and his deputies appeared, they looked shocked at Ernie's appearance, but Longarm had no time for their questions. "Ernie confessed that his brothers have kidnapped Nola Bugabee and they're keeping her at a farmhouse just east of town."

"How many brothers?"

"Three."

The marshal nodded with understanding. "All right, Custis, we'll go now and take all of my deputies but one."

"Sounds good. There's no time to waste. Get horses and let's ride."

Fifteen minutes later, Longarm and the grim Denver lawmen were galloping off to rescue Nola. Beside them, Ernie was tied to his saddle and almost unconscious with pain. Ruby had pleaded to be allowed to join them, but this time Longarm had been firm in his denying the request.

"We'll return in a couple of hours," he'd told the distraught woman. "If Nola is still alive, we'll get her back."

But now as they galloped across the flat plains of eastern Colorado, Longarm was thinking that saving Nola would be a lot more difficult than he'd first believed. Mainly, they would have trouble surprising the Haskill men because the land was open.

"We could wait for dark and sneak up on the farmhouse," one of the local deputies shouted over the pounding of their horses' hoofbeats. "That might be the smart thing."

Longarm had already considered and then discarded that strategy because, if bullets started flying, they'd likely kill Nola along with the Haskill brothers.

"We'll give them an ultimatum," Longarm shouted. "If they refuse to surrender, it probably means that they've already murdered Nola. If she's still alive, they ought to be able to see that it's suicidal to resist."

"What about me!" Ernie cried out. "When are you going to turn me loose?"

"We'll figure that out later," Longarm told the suffering man. "But if you've told me the whole truth, I will turn you loose."

Ernie seemed to take hope, and sat up a little straighter in his saddle. He was a fine rider, but the pounding of the running horses was taking its physical toll. Longarm knew that the man could not have ridden more than a few hours in his poor condition. As to the man's ultimate fate, Longarm just wasn't sure what he would do. He had told Ernie he could go free, or at least have the chance of a running start if he cooperated, but now Longarm was regretting that concession. Ernie was as guilty of kidnapping as any of the others, but Longarm had also needed his help and needed it in a big hurry.

"There it is!" Ernie shouted, pointing into the distance. "See those big cottonwood trees? The farmhouse is right among them."

Longarm judged the distance to be at least a mile. He drew his horse down to a walk and studied the lay of the land, hoping for a ditch or something that would offer cover for himself and the Denver lawmen.

There was nothing but flat, open farmland in every direction.

"All right, Custis, how are we going to handle this?" Leland asked, wiping sweat from his brow with a bandanna.

"We have no good choices," Longarm replied. "We'll

ride up as far as we dare and start yelling. They'll learn that we have Ernie and we want to exchange him for Nola."

"What!" Ernie cried in protest. "Please, you can't do that to me. My kinfolks will kill me for sure when they learn I've brought the law down on 'em."

"That's the best we can do," Longarm said with finality. "Once we have Nola and they've surrendered, you'll get your chance to make a run for your freedom."

"I'll have no chance," Ernie wailed. "Don't you understand what they'll do to me once I'm in their rifle sights?"

"If they kill you, they'll be murderers and probably hang," Longarm replied as they drew to within three hundred yards of the silent farmhouse. "I'll make sure they understand that fact."

Marshal Leland asked, "What if they refuse to turn the girl over to us, or she's dead and they won't surrender?"

"Then we surround the farmhouse and kill them all." Longarm drew his rifle from its saddle scabbard, and when he felt he was entering the killing range, he reined his horse to a standstill.

Longarm cupped his hands to his mouth and bellowed, "Clem, Bobby, and Earl Haskill. We have your brother and we want you to give us Nola Bugabee. Turn her loose and surrender or you're all going to die."

There was no answer.

One of the deputies said, "I don't see any saddle horses. Are we sure this is the right farmhouse?"

Longarm turned to Ernie for the answer to that question. "This is the right farmhouse, all right," said Ernie.

"What about the people who own the farm?" Leland demanded.

Ernie bit his lower lip, and finally stammered, "They . . . they were gone the first time we came here."

Longarm suddenly had a very bad feeling in the pit of his stomach. Farm people rarely left their homes because there was always livestock to feed. If the Haskills had murdered the owners, they would have nothing to gain by surrendering.

"What do we do now?" Ben Leland asked.

"We circle the farmhouse," Longarm told him. "When I fire a shot, we dismount and start moving in on them fast."

"That sounds pretty risky," a deputy said, looking worried.

"If you have a better plan," Longarm told the man, "then let's hear it right now."

"I still say we ought to wait for darkness."

But Longarm shook his head. "We'd kill Nola for sure, and that's not acceptable."

"All right," Leland said, "let's get moving. What about our prisoner?"

"He'll stay right here beside me," Longarm said. "The rest of you start moving."

Leland was the last to rein his horse away, but before he left, the lawman asked, "Do you really have any hope that the girl is still alive?"

"Not much," Longarm sadly admitted. "Not much at all."

Longarm waited beside Ernie until the lawmen had completely circled the trees and the farmhouse with its modest outbuildings. Then, he dismounted and told Ernie to do the same.

"What are you going to do?" the prisoner asked.

"We're going to start walking toward the house and keep telling them to surrender."

"But they won't do that!"

"Why not? Have they already killed Miss Bugabee?"

"How should I know! I'm not guilty of anything."

"Except helping to kidnap Nola and probably having a part in Boris's murder and torture. Now let's move!"

Longarm and Ernie started forward in plain view, and both had the same thought, that they'd jump behind their horses and use them as shields if the bullets started coming in their direction.

Longarm saw moving shadows in the doorway, and instinctively threw himself on the ground as two rifles opened fire. At the same time, Ernie started running toward the farmhouse yelling for them not to shoot him.

It didn't make any sense to Longarm to have one more Haskill to contend with, so he shot Ernie in the butt, dropping him about fifty yards from the front door of the farmhouse. Ernie howled and jumped up to run. Longarm levered another shell into his rifle and decided he was going to have to put Ernie Haskill down for keeps. He'd never shot a man in the back, but he'd be damned if he'd allow Ernie to reach his brothers as a reinforcement.

But just as Longarm was about to pull the trigger, one of Ernie's own brothers shot him while screaming, "Ernie, I'm sending you straight to hell for bringing the law down on us!"

Longarm could tell from the way that Ernie's body jerked and dropped that he was a dead man even before he hit the ground. At the same time, Longarm fired at the rifleman before he could duck back inside the farmhouse, and he heard the man cry that he was hit badly.

The lawmen from Denver opened fire from all sides, and Longarm saw them charge the farmhouse. Taking a deep breath, Longarm dropped his rifle, swung onto his horse, and set the animal running hard for the front door while trying to keep low in the saddle.

Bullets whip-cracked past his head, and Longarm thought he heard Nola scream, but he couldn't be sure because everything was happening so fast in the smoke and the confusion. As he neared the farmhouse, he leaned hard to his left, and then reined his mount so that it galloped past the door with very little of his body exposed to gunfire.

A bullet shattered his saddlehorn, and Longarm felt splinters of rawhide and leather cut at his right hand and wrist. He released his hold and struck the ground, rolling up against the farmhouse wall.

One of the Haskill brothers saw him and ran outside, which was a fatal mistake because Longarm had his gun up and fired almost point-blank into the man's body. Longarm jumped up and staggered toward the front door hearing glass shatter and Nola screaming. He bulled his way inside and saw muzzle flashes, and was just about to return fire when he heard a shout.

"Hold it!" Marshal Leland cried. "Don't shoot! It's over."

Longarm realized that he'd almost gunned down his friend. Now he could see Ben Leland standing in front of Nola protecting her from harm with his body.

"All dead?" Leland asked, his gun swinging back and forth in a slow, steady arc.

"I think so," Longarm replied.

"Marshal, look out!" Nola cried.

Longarm realized that he was wrong. The Haskill that he had shot in the doorway wasn't quite dead yet. Covered with blood but gritting his teeth and spitting oaths, the man had grabbed the edge of a chair, pulled himself erect, and fired at close range. Longarm heard the town marshal grunt as he swung his gun and emptied it into the last Haskill man standing.

"Ben, how badly are you hit?" Longarm shouted, running to his friend, who was already collapsing to the floor.

"I don't know," the man whispered, his voice already weak.

Ben Leland's deputies barged inside, and Longarm told them to help get their boss outside in the sunlight. Then, he turned to Nola, and saw at a glance that the poor girl had been put through a living hell.

"Come on," he said, taking her arm and leading her out with the others.

The deputies lay Ben down on a bed of leaves while Longarm tore the man's shirt and vest away to see exactly how badly he'd been shot.

As soon as the bullet hole was exposed, one of the deputies drew in a sharp breath and said, "It's real bad, isn't it, Marshal Long."

"It's not good," Longarm replied. "He's losing too much blood."

"Is he going to make it?"

"If I can stop the bleeding and if he hasn't been shot through some vital organ, then he has a fair chance," Longarm replied, figuring that he was being very optimistic. He'd seen a lot of gunshot wounds, and Ben's was one of those that could go either way. "Ride for town and bring out a doctor."

The deputy looked at Nola. "She's going to need a woman's help as well as a doctor's."

Longarm knew the deputy was right. Nola had obviously been beaten almost to death, and probably raped over and over by all three of the dead men. Her face was barely recognizable, and her hair was tangled with dirt and brush. One of her eyes was black and swollen shut, and her new dress had been torn, soiled, and sullied.

"Tell her sister, Ruby Bugabee, we need her here along with the doctor. And tell them both to come quick!"

The deputy sprinted for his horse, and was soon racing for Denver.

"He took the bullet that was meant for me," Nola said in a voice filled with wonder as she knelt beside Ben Leland. "He *shielded* my body with his body."

"That's right," Longarm agreed. "He definitely saved your life."

Nola bent low over the fallen lawman and whispered something in his ear. Whatever it was that she said, it seemed to help, because the marshal smiled and nodded with understanding.

"Here," Nola said, sitting up and tearing her dress for bandaging. "My dress ain't no good anymore. And I ain't any good anymore."

"You're going to be just fine, Nola. It's all over now and you're safe."

But Nola shook her head. "You *know* what they did to me, Custis. I'm no good no more."

Before Longarm could think of something . . . anything . . . that might make the girl feel better, Marshal Leland reached up and stroked her bruised cheek. "You're still good, Miss Bugabee," he insisted. "You're still a lady, and what happened here doesn't change a thing."

Nola hugged Ben's neck. Longarm would have left them like that, but he had to put a plug in Ben's wound so the man didn't bleed to death before a doctor arrived.

Longarm was good at plugging up bullet holes. He'd plugged up a few on himself as a last resort. Now, as Ben's deputies looked on anxiously, he used the strips that Nola tore from her new dress to pack and then bind the wound so tight that the bleeding seemed to stop.

"Am I going to make it?" the marshal asked. "Custis, as a friend I'm counting on you to tell me the truth."

"I think so," Longarm told him. "It just all depends on how much blood you have and how fast that doctor can get out here."

"It'll take him at least an hour," the marshal said, closing his eyes.

Nola leaned over and patted Ben's cheeks so that his eyes popped open. "You need to stay awake," she said. "You can't afford to drift off. Please stay awake because you're too good and brave to die."

"Water," Ben said, "I could use some water. My throat is real dry and I feel kind of hot."

Water was brought to the marshal, and as Longarm started to go check on the four dead Haskill men, he heard Nola tell the wounded marshal that he was the finest man she had ever known and that she would never forget how he risked his life to save her own. She also asked Ben Leland if he was a married man.

"No, Miss Bugabee, I've never gotten lucky enough to find a woman who'd have me as her husband," Leland replied.

"Then I'm thinking that both our lucks have just changed for the good," Nola told him.

Longarm didn't see it as he was walking away, but he would have sworn that heard the smack of a loud, wet kiss.

Chapter 6

It seemed to take a lot more than an hour before Longarm and the deputies saw a buggy come flying across the dry plains from the direction of Denver.

"That's Dr. Welch, and the woman must be Miss Bugabee's sister," one of the deputies observed as he whittled on a cottonwood branch.

The moment the buggy drew up under the cottonwoods, both the doctor and Ruby were hurrying to the wounded marshal and Nola, who had still not left her savior's side.

"Oh, Nola!" Ruby cried when she saw how badly her sister had been treated. "Are you all right?"

Tears formed in Nola's eyes and ran down her bruised and swollen cheeks. "Ruby," she whispered, "they treated me like a whore and I thought they were gonna kill me. And . . . and I'm ashamed to say that they made me tell them everything I remembered about our half of the map!"

"That doesn't matter," her older sister replied. "You're still alive and that's all that counts right now."

"But I told them everything about the Arizona gold!"

"I don't care," Ruby said, hugging her sister tightly. "I thought sure that you were dead."

While Dr. Welch examined Ben Leland, Longarm took the opportunity to have a word with Nola when she had calmed down in her sister's arms. "What about Jude and his brothers and cousins?" he asked. "Do you know how many were in that bunch that has already left for Arizona?"

Nola took a deep breath. "Clem Haskill spoke of Jude and a couple of others that already have Boris's half of the map, but he never said exactly how many were already on their way to Picacho Peak."

"What else can you tell me?"

"Clem said that they were going to kill me if I didn't help them get the other part of the map, and they had to have it before Jude would allow them to leave Denver. Then Bobby said that they were all going to get rich in Arizona and maybe buy a cattle ranch down there and never go back to West Virginia. I had the feeling they had done something wrong to their own folks back in West Virginia before leaving."

"They probably robbed from them to get the money to come West," Longarm said. "That wouldn't surprise me. I expect Jude and his bunch were thrown out by their own clan because they got too lawless."

"Nola," Ruby said, changing the subject, "I'm so sorry about what happened to you."

"Well, at least it happened to me and not you. It's not like I was a virgin, you know."

"Listen," Ruby said, trying to sound as if none of that mattered, "neither of us have been virgins since we were thirteen years old, but that don't make what Clem and those boys did right. And they had no call to beat you up."

She turned to Longarm. "Are all three dead?"

"Yes. And Ernie Haskill. We were damned lucky to get to Nola before they killed her. I just hope that Marshal Leland will pull through."

"I'll just die if he don't!" Nola exclaimed. "That man stepped in front of me and took my bullet. He saved my life."

Longarm knew that was true. "Ben Leland is one of the finest lawmen I have ever met. He's been risking his life for others a long, long time. He is a hero, Nola."

The young woman reached out to squeeze Longarm's hand. "You are too, Custis. We'd heard that you were famous, and now I can see why."

Longarm wasn't one to bask in his own accomplishments, so he left the two sisters and went back to see what the doctor had to say about the condition of his friend, who was pale and looking as if he might die at any moment.

"Hang on, Ben!" Longarm urged. "Doc?"

"We'll put the marshal in my buggy and drive real slow," Dr. Welch told everyone as he walked over to join them where they'd gathered under the cottonwoods. "Marshal Leland's blood has coagulated, but the clot could break loose if the marshal suffers too much jarring on the way back to town."

"What about the bullet?" Longarm asked. "Doc, I didn't see an exit wound."

Dr. Welch stroked his goatee. He was a man in his sixties, large and rotund, with an air of competency and vigor, but he also looked grim. "I'm eventually going to have to remove the bullet. When I do, it will cause even more loss of blood, so we won't do that surgery for a few days, while the marshal builds up his strength."

"What are his chances?"

"I don't know," the doctor admitted. "If I can get that bullet out of him and he doesn't bleed to death internally, then he'll make it. If not . . ."

Longarm understood. "I've got to go after Jude Haskill and his men, so I can't be here when you operate. But I want you to do your best and take good care of him."

"I will," Welch said. "But Ben's outcome in not only in my hands . . . but in God's. Your prayers might help."

"I'm not much of a man for prayer," Longarm confessed. "The best thing I can do is to catch up with the Haskill bunch and put a stop to them before they take it upon themselves to murder any more innocent folks. And they'll do that whenever they need money or fresh horses. That's why there's no time to lose in taking up the hunt."

"I understand. But you are a federal marshal and this is a *local* crime. What is your authority in this matter?"

"It doesn't matter because what the Haskill men have done to my cousins goes beyond legal matters," Longarm told the doctor.

"I understand and wish you well," Welch said as he hurried back to the side of his patient.

Unknown to Longarm, Ruby had come up behind him to listen to the conversation. When Longarm turned to go to his horse, Ruby said, "I'm going with you after the Haskill bunch."

"No."

"I *have* to go with you."

"Ruby, you need to stay here and help your sister recover both physically and in her mind."

"She'll heal strong with or without me. Besides, Nola just said that she's fallen in love with Marshal Leland, who she learned is still a bachelor."

"He is, but Dr. Welch says he could die of his bullet wound."

"All the more reason for Nola to stay by his side."

Longarm checked his cinch. "Listen, Ruby, you know what I'm going up against. Jude is leading the pack of Haskills, but we aren't sure how many. You and your sister said that three of them left West Virginia, but now we know there were at least seven. There may be even more."

74

"I realize the odds aren't good for us, but I'm a crack shot."

Longarm wasn't impressed. "Shooting squirrels for the soup pot isn't the same as getting into a gunfight."

"I won't quit on you and my nerve won't break," Ruby vowed.

"I can't allow it."

Ruby Bugabee looked him right in the eye and said, "And you can't stop it, Custis. I'm going to Arizona . . . with or without you."

"And do you really think you'd have any chance against Jude and his brothers?"

"Probably not."

Longarm shook his head. "All right," he said, "I expect that you can borrow Ben Leland's horse for our trip to Arizona. He won't be needing a saddle animal for a while, and I'm sure he'll be wanting us to put an end to the Haskills."

Ruby's eyes widened. "You're really going to let me go with you?"

"I am. We'll ride along with the Doc and his buggy into town. You can get Nola settled in and comfortable, but only if you're sure she'll be all right without you."

"She'll do fine. I know she wants to stay near the marshal, and besides, she won't be fit to travel for a while." Ruby choked back a sob as she thought about what had happened to her younger sister. "Custis?"

He put his arms around her. "Yeah?"

"Nola is a *good* woman, but she's no saint and neither am I."

"None of us are, Ruby. You don't need to make apologies. I've done more than my share of wrongs and I've killed more men that I care to remember."

Ruby looked up at him. "You're strong, just like the rest of the Long men . . . most of whom were killed in the war. When Nola and I set out from West Virginia, we were so scared of what we'd come across that we just kept telling ourselves that Marshal Custis Long—our strong and fearless cousin—was out in Colorado. We knew that if we could just get this far west and find you, everything would be all right."

Longarm felt an ache in his throat. "I wish that had been true," he managed to say. "But you *did* find me, and look what happened to Boris and Nola. I'm afraid you overrated my ability because I couldn't protect either one of them from the Haskills."

"Let's go get even with those bastards, Custis! It doesn't matter to me anymore if we find a treasure or not. I just want to pay them back for what they did to Boris and Nola."

"Me too," Longarm said. "Do you see that sorrel gelding over there?"

"Yes."

"That's the marshal's horse. Go adjust the stirrups and check the cinch to make sure it's good and tight. Jude and his bunch are days ahead of us, but I know every shortcut there is through the Rocky Mountains, and I figure we can cut the distance."

"Do you think we can overtake them before they reach Picacho Peak?"

"Depends on how much hell they raise on their way," Longarm said as he went over to tell the marshal that Ruby intended to borrow his horse for a month or two.

"You're what!" Billy Vail exclaimed in his handsome office.

"I'm turning down your offer for travel expenses," Longarm told his boss for the second time. "And I'm handing in my badge."

Billy vaulted out of his desk chair with a lot more agility than Longarm had given him credit for. "Custis, you can't do that!"

"I can't *not* do it."

"But why?"

"Because," Longarm told his longtime boss and friend, "when we catch up to Jude Haskill and his brothers, I mean to kill them to the last damn man."

Billy blinked and plopped back down in his desk chair. "What you're telling me is that you mean to *execute* the Haskill brothers."

"You can use that word if it suits you," Longarm snapped. "But they'll also be trying to kill me and Ruby."

"You're making a huge mistake."

"I've made plenty and I'll make plenty more before I'm through."

"Custis, listen to me for once."

"I listen to you all the time."

"But *really* listen this time."

Billy took a deep breath and composed himself as he considered his next words. "If you resign from office, you'll just be another man out there with vengeance in his heart. And even if you are successful in pulling off this blood vendetta, you'll most likely be charged with murder."

"Why?"

"Because we have courts of law!" Billy shouted. "We *suspect* that Jude Haskill and the men riding with him tortured and murdered Boris Bugabee, but we don't yet have *proof*."

"I don't need proof."

"You do unless you want to be charged with murder."

Longarm didn't want to hear this.

"Custis, you can't just ride after these men and gun them down like animals. If you do that, you'll be charged with murder, and even if you're acquitted, I'll never be able to hire you back as a federal officer."

"Then I'm damned if I do . . . and damned if I don't."

"No! Just keep your badge and your authority and I'll

put out a warrant for their arrest on the suspicion of the murder of Boris Bugabee. After which, you can go after that bunch with the full authority and privilege of a United States marshal. Do you see what the difference is here?"

"I guess."

"Of course you do," Billy said. "As a badge-carrying officer who has been sworn to protect the citizens of this country and uphold its laws, you have the authority to go after Jude and his brothers and use whatever force is required to bring them to justice."

"But if I turn in my badge, I'm just a bounty hunter."

"Not even that," Billy told him, "because there is no bounty on their heads that I'm aware of."

"Will you swear out a warrant for their arrest even without proof?"

"I'll get a judge to do that."

"How long with it take?" Longarm asked. "Every minute that I sit is another minute that separates me from Jude."

Billy came to his feet. "If you promise not to turn in your badge, then I'll promise you to have the arrest warrant and your three hundred dollars of travel money in one hour or less."

"Fair enough," Longarm said, realizing that he was being offered something very unusual and that Billy was really sticking out his neck in the name of friendship.

"And one more thing I'll promise," Billy said. "I'll be checking up on Miss Bugabee and Marshal Leland every day and offering whatever help they might need."

"That would be greatly appreciated."

"Where is Miss Bugabee staying?"

Longarm told him the name of her boardinghouse.

"I know an old lady who could use some help doing light housekeeping and cleaning," Billy said. "She would give Miss Bugabee free room and board and also a small salary. Is your country cousin up to that?"

"It might be just what the doctor ordered," Longarm said. "Nola has been violated and she's pretty beat up. I'm sure she'll want to stay out of the public, and she is dead broke."

"This old lady is sweet and she'll treat Miss Bugabee like a daughter—that is, providing the girl is clean and honest."

"She's a little on the rough side and lacking in manners and tact," Longarm admitted, "but Nola is honest and I have the feeling she'll try hard to please."

"Then why don't I see if I can make the arrangements today?" Billy asked. "Where can I find Miss Bugabee right this moment?"

"My guess is that she'll be wherever Marshal Leland is recovering."

Billy's eyebrows lifted in question. "Is she . . . taken with Ben?"

"That's understating it."

"My goodness. Ben Leland is a confirmed bachelor."

Longarm managed a smile. "Sure, but he's never met a determined young girl from the backwoods of West Virginia. I could be wrong, but if our marshal survives his wound, he's going to be cooked meat on Nola Bugabee's table."

Billy laughed. "She sounds like quite a gal. What's her older sister like?"

Longarm's smile faded. "Right now, Ruby is as filled with anger as I am and bent on nothing but revenge."

"I wish you weren't taking her along with you to Arizona."

"Me too, but she won't take no for an answer. And besides, Ruby assures me that she is a sharpshooter."

"And what *else* is she?"

Longarm didn't miss the emphasis on the word "else," and he knew what Billy was thinking. "Forget that. We're in this for one thing, and that's to stop Jude Haskill and his brothers permanently."

"Good," Billy said. "It would do you well to remember that. By the way, are you still taking the train down to Pueblo?"

"I was thinking we might just ride hard and maybe catch up with the Haskill bunch."

"Bad idea. Why don't you take horses but put them in boxcars heading south?"

Longarm shrugged. "Pretty damned expensive to rent an entire boxcar for just two horses."

"I know someone who works for the railroad. If there are some empty cattle cars going south, you could be in Pueblo in four or five hours. If you rode that far it would take two days."

"Good point."

"Want me to go over and see?"

Longarm had to smile because he knew Billy wanted to get some fresh air. But the offer was very tempting. The Haskill men would most likely have ridden south through Pueblo and then over Raton Pass into New Mexico before turning west. "I'd sure appreciate that," Longarm said. "It would help us catch up in a hurry."

"Good. We'll go over to the railroad after I return with that arrest warrant and your travel money," Billy promised, rushing off with a look that told Longarm the man could not be denied.

Chapter 7

Longarm and Ruby got lucky and managed not only to get to Pueblo, but clear down to Santa Fe on the Atchison–Topeka–Santa Fe line. But the trouble was they had to stay with their horses in cattle cars all the way down.

"I sure will be glad to get out of this stinking cattle car," Ruby said, her new dress stained green with cow and horse manure. "What time do you think it is?"

Longarm figured it was well past midnight. They had been riding in cattle cars for two days, and it was the most miserable trip of his entire life. He'd almost been gored by a frisky longhorn cow while the train had labored over Raton Pass, and it had been cold at that high altitude. Then, the marshal's horse had tromped on Ruby's new shoes, and she believed that at least three of her toes were crushed.

"We'll get off at Santa Fe and get hot baths and new clothes," Longarm promised. "And a good meal."

"And new shoes. These fancy ones you bought for us in Denver are worthless around horses. And a bed. Neither one of us has slept a wink since we left Denver," Ruby complained. "I'm so tired I could sleep for a week. How far have we come on this damned train?"

"About four hundred miles," Longarm told her. "On horseback riding hard, it would have taken a good nine or ten days to get this far south."

"Then we're probably ahead of Jude and his bunch."

"No doubt," Longarm told her. "And there is a fair chance he and his brothers will pass through Santa Fe. We'll contract the marshal and see if he can help us."

"Those boys won't surrender," Ruby promised. "I expect you remember Jude as being crazy and full of hell."

"I remember him as being crazy, cunning, and mean," Longarm said. "And I expect he's gotten worse."

"He has," Ruby said, huddling close to Longarm and peering through the slats of the banging, rattling cattle car. "Do you think our horses are going to be any good after what we've been through these past two days?"

"I expect so," Longarm told her. "We'll put them up in a livery for a day or two of rest. That and good feed will bring them around."

"They don't act too perky now. Heads hanging down and all covered with cow shit."

"We probably look even worse," Longarm said. "I have to tell you, Ruby, this is the sorriest I've ever felt or looked. I'm halfways ashamed to step off the train, and I sure hope it gets to Santa Fe before daylight so folks can't see us climb out of this boxcar."

"Me too."

"But it'll be worth it if we've gotten ahead of Jude. He'll be expecting me to be on his backtrail, but we'll be waiting in Santa Fe with some of the town's lawmen."

"You told me that they might have gone straight over the mountains. If they did, we've lost them until we reach Picacho Peak, and that's still a little ways off, ain't it?"

"More than a little, I'm afraid."

"How much farther?" Ruby demanded.

"I'm not sure," Longarm hedged, not wanting to further discourage the woman from West Virginia. "But it's still a fair piece."

"Custis, you got any cigars left?"

"Two."

"Why don't we smoke 'em up seein' as how we can get more in Santa Fe."

"Good idea."

Longarm dragged out the cigars from his coat pocket. The livestock cars that they were riding in were six inches deep in manure, and he was hoping that the strong cigars would kill the stench even if just for a half hour or so. But when he lit the first cigar for Ruby, one of the longhorns spooked, and that sent the entire bunch into a shoving match as they milled around in the cattle car.

"Holy flying shit!" Longarm shouted, leaping up on the side of the car as Ruby did the same, both of them staring down into the semidarkness at the cattle and their horses.

"They're probably goring our horses to death right now," Ruby said. "Tell me again why we had to ride back here with these damned spooky cattle."

"Railroad rules," Longarm explained for at least the fiftieth time. "The railroad engineer said it wouldn't be right to let us ride in the passenger cars since we already got to put our horses on board for free."

"Well," Ruby said, "I'd rather Jude shoot holes in me when we meet up with him than to have to come back this same way. I just won't do it, Custis!"

"Me neither," he said, wishing he hadn't dropped the cigar and that the longhorns would settle down so they could climb off the sides of the cattle car they were clinging to. "This whole thing is a disgrace. If I ever get back to Denver, I'm going to throttle Billy Vail for suggesting we do this."

"I'll help you."

•   •   •

Dawn was just breaking on the horizon when their train finally dragged into Santa Fe. Then, they had to wait another half hour for the railroad men to get around to the cattle cars before they could unload their horses and finally stand on solid ground.

"It's a fine morning," Ruby said, "but judging from the way that those railroad fellas stared at us, we're not lookin' too fine."

"I can say for certain that *you* aren't," Longarm replied, gaping at Ruby, who was covered with a layer of crud composed of soot from the train, cinders from the railroad bed, manure from the livestock, and dust from everywhere. It appeared to be about a half-inch thick on her Ruby's face, and he couldn't help laugh.

"What is so damned funny!"

"If you could just see yourself now!" Longarm cackled.

The woman was exhausted, in pain, but Longarm's laughter was contagious. "I don't need to see myself because I can see *you*!"

Standing on the train platform at dawn and holding their half-dead horses, they laughed and laughed, but when their lunacy finally ran its course, they mounted their horses and trotted into the town. Santa Fe was old, and one of Longarm's favorite places to visit, but he sure wasn't eager to meet up with any of his past acquaintances. It was still early, roosters were crowing, and there were very few people up and about, but Longarm knew that would soon change.

"I know a little out-of-the-way hotel where we can hole up in for a while," Longarm said. "It's cheap, and the owner won't give us any problems about how crappy we look."

"We should take care of the horses first," Ruby reminded him.

"I know that, but let's clean up and get some decent

clothes before we find a livery. Our horses can stand at a hitching rail for a few hours."

Ruby shook her head. "We were taught to always take care of our animals first. I know your pappy also taught you that, so let's do it before we get to the hotel."

Ruby pointed at her horse's head, which was hanging nearly to the ground. "Look at this poor beast! He's out on his feet and covered with muck the same as we are. He ain't been properly watered or fed in two days. It's not right to make him wait at a hitching rail."

"It wouldn't bother me to let him wait an hour."

"I won't hear of it!" Ruby insisted. "After all, a horse has pride in its appearance just like we do."

"Oh, bull!" Longarm said, but he was feeling guilty because he knew that Ruby was right about taking care of your animals before yourself. "All right then, we'll do it."

"Good," Ruby said. "That appears to be a livery just up the street. We can turn them into a corral and make sure they're watered and fed properly, then feel right about taking care of ourselves."

"Fine," Longarm snapped, in no mood to be lectured.

"What in the hell happened to you!" the liveryman cried, dropping the pitchfork he was using to pitch hay to a corral full of horses.

"We had a long ride in a cattle car all the way down from Denver," Longarm told the man. "And it isn't healthy to laugh at us."

The liveryman heard the edge in Longarm's voice, and clamped his mouth shut in a hurry.

"Take these horses and make sure that they're grained and well fed," Longarm told the man. "I want them put into stalls or a separate corral. They're too tired to fight a corral full of horses over hay."

"Cost you a dollar a day in private stalls."

"For the pair?"

"No," the man said, "each."

"That's outrageous!" Ruby cried.

"Take it or leave it," the man said. "I got plenty of business right here in Santa Fe, and I'll have to charge you extra to wash and then curry those horses. Given that they're coated with cow shit, it'll be a hard chore for one of my boys."

Longarm wasn't tight with money, but he didn't like to get stuck either. "Maybe we should find another livery," he said.

"Suit yourself," the man told him. "But my prices are as cheap as anyone's and I feed a better quality of hay."

Longarm saw two women stop in the street and gape at him and Ruby. He saw their hands fly to their mouths, either in astonishment that two human beings could be so filthy, or else to prevent themselves from laughing out loud. Longarm couldn't be sure which reaction the women were experiencing, but either way it got his dander up.

"All right, you win!" he snapped, shoving his reins into the liveryman's calloused hands.

"I get paid in advance," the man had the nerve to add. "If you please."

Longarm almost hit the man, but managed to control himself and extract five dollars from his pocket. He gathered his saddlebags and Winchester before they hurried off down the street to the hotel he was thinking about, where they could get cleaned and rested up before they faced Jude Haskill and his brothers.

"Marshal Long?" the Mexican who owned the little adobe hotel on the outskirts of Santa Fe asked, his face showing disbelief.

"That's right, it's me."

"But what happened to your face? And your clothes? And . . . and is this a *señorita*?"

"We'll explain later," Longarm said. "We need two

86

rooms. One for the lady and one for myself. And baths as soon as you can get the water heated."

Juan Escobar nodded with understanding, and he knew Longarm well enough not to ask for payment in advance. "I will give you the room on the patio by the fountain. The same one you had last time you were here with a lady."

"That's fine," Longarm said, trying to remember who he'd brought here last. "And I think you had better give the lady a room next to mine."

"Of course, Señor Long! Two rooms on the patio and then two hot baths."

"Prepare the lady's bath first," Longarm said.

"And something to eat and drink in your rooms?"

"Yes, please." Longarm remembered that Juan had a very special taste for excellent tequila. He probably had it brought in by his relatives down in Mexico. In any case it was first-rate, and the idea of tequila, a little lemon, and salt was suddenly very appealing. "Your special tequila would be *muy bueno*."

"*Sí!*"

Juan shouted some orders that Longarm knew would be heard from the kitchen. He showed them to their adjoining rooms, and scurried off to encourage his family members to make haste.

"These rooms are beautiful," Ruby said as she surveyed the bright bedspread and the Spanish gourds and pottery that decorated both rooms. There were roses in the vases and potted plants on the shelves. "And I've never seen such a fine floor."

"It's *saltillo* tile imported from the Mexican state of Sonora," Longarm told her. "The Mexican people are exceptional with rock, tile, and they love flowers and bright colors. I'm glad you like it."

"I'm afraid to touch anything because it's all so clean and pretty."

Longarm nodded with understanding. He would not have dreamed of sitting in one of the handsome chairs or on his bedspread.

"I won't be able to stand up for long," Ruby said. "My legs feel as heavy as oak logs and my eyelids feel as if they are weighted down by rocks."

"Mine too. We'll bathe and then Juan will have some tortillas, cheese, and salsa brought to our rooms along with the tequila. Then we'll sleep through the morning, and see what we can find out this afternoon."

"That sounds like a wonderful plan," Ruby told him. "And the idea of a hot bath sounds best of all."

Longarm couldn't have agreed more. He was almost certain that Jude and his brothers were still somewhere between Pueblo and Santa Fe, and that they would not arrive in this old trading center for at least another couple of days.

And in the meantime, it was a good chance to rest up and have a little fun showing Ruby the town and the entertainment spots that he'd often frequented on his trips through this part of New Mexico.

What the hell, Longarm thought. *We could be killed when we finally do have our showdown, and we might as well live it up a bit first.*

"Custis?"

"Yeah?"

"You don't think there's any chance that Jude is already here and that he might find us sleeping in our beds and kill us, do you?"

"No. Juan and his family never let anyone into this patio where all the best rooms face. It's safe and secluded. So you can rest easy and sleep sound. Besides, I'll be right next door."

"I know that," she said. "And the next time you see me

I'll look like a real woman again instead of a walking, talking fountain of cow shit."

"So will I," Longarm said with a laugh as they separated, each trying to remember how fine the other had looked when they'd left Denver.

Chapter 8

They had bathed and slept well through the heat of the day, and it was nearly five o'clock when Longarm heard a soft knock at his door and sat up in his bed.

"Come on in."

Ruby appeared wearing a blue and red serape and a blush on her cheeks. "Juan's wife Rosita let me borrow this until she could get my dress washed and dried. I had nothing else to wear."

"Yeah," Longarm said as he stifled a yawn. "They took my clothes and washed them this morning too. I don't think they can get them clean of all those manure stains, but they might surprise us both. They wash and scrub everything on a smooth stone out near the fountain."

Ruby came inside and sat down in Longarm's bedside chair. "We've slept all day and I feel alive again."

"I expect I will too when I fully awaken."

"Is it too late to go see the local marshal and tell him about Jude and his brothers?"

Longarm consulted his Ingersoll watch, which had a fine gold chain. Ordinarily, the chain would have been attached to a watch fob, but Longarm's chain was soldered to a solid-brass, twin-barreled derringer.

"How interesting!" Ruby said. "Mind if I look at it?"

"Nope, but it is loaded."

"Why do you have your watch attached to a derringer?"

"There have been a few times when that watch and derringer saved my life. You see, a man might get the drop on you and get your six-gun, but he'd rarely think to worry about a derringer attached to your watch chain."

Ruby held the pocket watch in one hand and the .44 caliber derringer in the other. After a few moments, she mused aloud, "I'm holding life as reflected in time and death reflected in a gun." She glanced up at Longarm. "Kind of an odd and interesting balance and connection, don't you think?"

"I've never quite thought of it like that, but you're right. Interesting that you should see that connection, Ruby."

His remark had been meant as a compliment, but Ruby took it as a slight.

"I may not be well educated or sophisticated, but I'm not stupid. When you grow up in the woods, you usually have time to sit and think about a lot of things. Time to watch and learn and listen. I don't think that city people do much watching or listening. In Denver, they all seemed to be in such a big hurry to get someplace or do something. And I doubt any of them have watched birds, coons, or swam in a pond."

"That's true," Longarm said. "I know that I don't get the chance to do any of those slow-and-easy things that I did as a kid back in West Virginia."

"Why did you ever leave us?"

"The war. I was just sick of the killing and I wanted to go someplace fresh and clean. That meant the American West."

"And you have no desire to ever go back home?"

"Home to me now is Denver. I like the city, and the

Rocky Mountains are more rugged and tougher than the Appalachians."

"And that's good?" Ruby asked.

"It's neither good nor bad. It's just that I've grown to like the West and the openness of its landscape. I'd feel all crowded in if I were back in the East again with those endless heavy forests. Now I prefer vistas and long shadows from clouds that move across the open ground. I favor and savor sunsets and sunrises that can be seen from a hundred miles in any direction."

"I guess you are a Westerner now," Ruby said. "But I mean to get that gold from Arizona and get back to our home. I know that Nola feels exactly the same way."

"I hope there is a treasure," Longarm said. "It sounds as if your people could use some help."

"They sure could. Backwoods folks are poor and they don't have much hope when it comes to money. As you know, we farm as hard as we can on poor soil, and we collect coal to keep us from freezing in the mean, wet winters. We catch fish and hunt. Now and then, we might even make a little extra money working for someone, but it never lasts for long. In the Eastern cities, they see backwoods folks as being slothful and ignorant."

"That's not true and it never has been," Longarm said. "Our families are uneducated and often out of touch with what is going on outside their little towns and villages, but they work hard and they care about each other in a way that you won't find in the West."

"That's right." Ruby told him. "Nola and I had reached exactly the same conclusions. Poor Nola. I just hope that she can get over what those animals did to her at that farmhouse. And I'm very worried that the marshal will die of his wound."

"Dr. Welch is a fine doctor. If anyone in Denver can save Marshal Ben Leland, he can."

"Nola seemed happy with her situation when we left

her," Ruby said. "I think she's going to be fine, especially if she and Ben Leland spend much time together."

Longarm caught her drift. "Nola shouldn't get her hopes up about snagging Ben for a husband. He's always been successful in outrunning women who had marrying on their minds."

"That may be true, but you don't know my sister," Ruby countered. "She's quieter than me, but she's a real charmer. And when she sets her mind to getting something, it gets got."

Longarm was enjoying himself, but wondering how he was going to get out of bed since he was stark naked under the bedspread and covers.

As if she could read his mind, Ruby said, "You're not wearing a stitch, are you, Cousin Custis?"

"Not a stitch," he confessed.

"I don't mind if you get up and get some clothes," Ruby told him. "I've seen naked men before. My father was the first, but I got lots of brothers that ran around naked when it was warm, and I have been with men."

"Many?" Longarm could have cut out his tongue for asking. It was none of his business and not the kind of question a man asked his cousin.

But Ruby didn't seem at all embarrassed. "Let's see, first there was Jethro Talbot, when I was down at the creek and he found me swimmin' without a stitch. Then there was Eddie and his brother, Claude Hicks. Claude was a man, and he had to show Eddie what to do with what little he had to use on me. It was funny, and I started to giggling, but Eddie got so upset he ran away. So Claude and me did it all one afternoon in the grass."

Ruby blushed. "This must sound just terrible! I shouldn't be tellin' you about all the men and boys I've enjoyed."

Longarm was beginning to have some shameful thoughts about his cousin.

"Custis?" she asked.

"Yeah?"

"Who did you bring into this room?"

"I've forgotten."

Ruby's eyebrows lifted with surprise. "Are you tellin' me that you made love to a woman here and you can't even remember her name or nothin'?"

"It's the truth and I feel ashamed," he told her, although he really did not. "I probably met some woman in a cantina and we came back here after drinking and dancing."

"Does that happen to you very often?"

"Not as often as I'd like," he said with a chuckle. "But I'm not complaining."

"Maybe *that's* why you like it out here," Ruby said in a tone of voice that indicated his words were a real revelation. "You know that doesn't happen much in the backwoods of West Virginia."

"Nope, and when a man does take a girl, he'd better be damned careful, or her family will either kill him or insist they get hitched."

"That's right." Ruby shook her head. "I don't understand why it's so different from where we grew up compared to out West. We're all Americans, ain't we?"

"Of course we are, but families aren't tight-knit out West. Everyone is always running off someplace, and people rarely live in one town or city for years and years. They're always on the move. In most cases, Westerners are more rootless and restless than the folks back East, who sometimes never go more than a few miles from where they were born during their entire lifetimes."

Ruby thought about that for several minutes. "I never expected to come to the West, and neither did Nola. But we knew about you being a famous marshal, and we'd always wonder what you were up to. We'd make up and then act out exciting fights and shootings and pretend. Nola and I would take turns on who would be Marshal

Custis Long and who would be an outlaw. We'd even practice fast-drawing wooden guns we'd carved, and whoever was the outlaw you gunned down had to die hard."

"You're serious?" Longarm was amazed.

"I sure am. We played being you and an outlaw all the time. It was fun."

"I'm flattered."

"You ought to be, Custis. You see, to us, and I think to most of the family, you'd done something more exciting than anyone else had ever done. Our folks and family used to talk about you all the time, and once . . . we even had you backing down Wild Bill Hickok."

Longarm gave a loud belly laugh. "Well," he said, "I'm *not* famous, and I sure never backed Wild Bill down. But I have had some bad fights. I've been shot, stabbed, and knocked out cold. I've got scars all over my body."

"Can I see a bullet wound and a knife wound?"

Longarm wasn't sure that this was such a smart idea. "The knife wound is here on my side," he said, pulling back the bedspread so that it covered him just from the waist down. "But my worst bullet wound is lower than a female cousin should see on a man."

"Oh, come on!"

"All right," Longarm decided, "but I've warned you."

He drew back the bedspread, and showed Ruby a bullet wound that he'd caught in the groin while chasing a bank robber and his accomplices down on the Pecos River. It had almost been the death of him, and it would have been if there hadn't been an Army surgeon close at hand.

"My gosh!" Ruby said, staring first at the wound and then at something very much different. "That's huge!"

"Oh, it was a .50-caliber ball that struck me and just . . ."

Longarm suddenly realized that Ruby wasn't staring at his bullet wound. No, sir, she was staring at his rod, and with more than a casual, cousinly interest. He started to pull the bedspread back over his lower half, but she stopped him, and the next thing he knew, Ruby was on the bed and she had his manhood firmly clasped in his hand.

"This is bigger than any I've held before. Why, most of the fish I've caught in the creeks with a cane pole wouldn't measure up to this monster. Can you make it even larger?"

"Ruby," Longarm protested, gently trying to push her away. "We're *relatives*."

"Kind of distant relatives," she whispered.

"Not so distant," he said with a dry mouth.

Ruby swallowed hard and tore off her borrowed serape. "Distant enough!"

The next thing he knew, she was all over him, kissing and hugging and tugging at his manhood until it was fully extended.

"We shouldn't do this being as we're cousins," he grunted as she spread her legs wide and engulfed him in her hot, sweet honey pot.

"Well, Cousin Custis, we're doing it and I sure ain't complaining!"

Ruby was strong, and she was totally without inhibitions. She'd seen animals couple all her life; dogs, cats, horses, cows, and pigs. She'd probably been watching them since she was in diapers, and later, when she was still just a girl, she'd just naturally wanted to see what the excitement was all about.

Now, she was a woman and there was plenty of excitement, to Longarm's way of thinking. And although he figured it was sinful as sinful could get, he couldn't stop once they got started . . . hell, he didn't even want to stop.

"Come on! Come on!" she cried, bouncing up and down on him as fast as she could with her lips drawn back and her eyes wide open. "Oh my oh my, Cousin Custis, I wish you'd been home all these years! I'd have found out about this big thing of yours and we'd have had a great time. Nola would have discovered it too, and the two of us would have worn you down to a sore, red nubbin!"

Longarm grabbed her hips and drove himself in and out of Ruby with all the power he could muster. She had large breasts, and they were bouncing up and down, and this was more fun than he'd had since he'd been with Olivia. Hell, this was even more fun than Olivia!

He rolled her over and rode her hard until she was half crazed with the feeling, and when Ruby began to scream, Longarm had to clamp his hand over her mouth because he knew that Juan Escobar and his wife and mother-in-law would start howling with laughter at all the commotion that was going on in Longarm's room.

"Oh, Mr. Marshal, you are wonderful!" Ruby screamed through the seams of his fingers as she fell forward and his body exploded sending his hot seed into the depths of her strong mountain-born-and-bred body.

"Dear Kissin' Cousin Custis," she gasped, hugging him tight and fighting for breath between kisses. "I sure hope that Jude don't show up for a while 'cause . . . until he does . . . we're gonna have us a *real* good time!"

As Longarm vigorously gave her his last sticky drop, he couldn't have agreed more.

Chapter 9

Longarm was getting worried and restless after a week in old Santa Fe. Sure, he was enjoying Ruby's company, and after that first day they'd moved into the same room, but where were Jude and the other Haskill men?

"Maybe," Longarm said to Ruby late one sunny morning, "I've misjudged this thing and they went straight west over the Rocky Mountains out of Denver. If they did, I've made a real miscalculation."

Ruby was sitting beside a fountain in the enclosed patio admiring the flowers and garden. "It's so beautiful in here that I wish we could stay forever. The town of Santa Fe itself is nice, but I feel like we're in a world of our own right here in this garden."

"It is relaxing," Longarm agreed, "but sitting here enjoying the flowers and fountain isn't getting anything done. Jude and his brothers should have been in Santa Fe by now."

"What else can be done? We've gone to see the local marshal every day and he's got his deputies watching for Jude."

"We could ride north toward Raton Pass," Longarm said. "Maybe intercept the Haskills."

"But if they came south, you said that they'd almost surely pass through Santa Fe."

"I know," Longarm replied, "but I'm not one to sit around. I'm a man who craves action."

Ruby smiled. "I thought I was giving you all the action you could handle day and night."

Longarm's face relaxed. "Believe me, you are. I've no complaints about that, but we can't afford to wait much longer. If they've already turned west and headed for Durango or Cortez, we could wait here forever and never catch them."

"It's a long way back up to Raton Pass."

"Yeah," he said, "too far to backtrack."

Ruby came over to stand beside him. "Let's give it one or two more days and then ride straight for Arizona."

"Thats sounds good to me," Longarm said. "But I'm feeling kind of cooped up and I'd like to get out of town for a while. Let's ask Juan's wife to pack us a picnic lunch. We can ride up in the hills and spend the day."

"I'd like that very much."

So it was decided, and Longarm immediately felt in better spirits. He never had been one to sit around more than a few days, and their horses could also use the exercise.

They had ridden only ten or twelve miles, but found a nice stream and trees where they could be shaded through the afternoon. Besides the food and a few bottles of beer that were packed in their saddlebags, Longarm had brought a blanket, and now, as they finished off their tortillas, meat, and second beers, which they'd chilled in the stream, Longarm was relaxed and even sleepy.

"I'm glad we got out of town for the day," he told Ruby as he stretched out on the blanket and closed his eyes, his head resting in her lap. "It's a fine old town, but a fella could spend a lot of money, and I never was a great one for shopping."

Ruby gazed down at her new pants, blouse, and boots. "You have spent a lot of money on clothes for us. I hope you aren't going broke."

"Don't worry about it," Longarm said. "We had to have new clothes after what we went through in those cattle cars. Besides, you needed things that you could use on the trail, and dresses just won't work."

"I'm used to wearing men's clothes. But I sort of miss my straw hat."

"I don't," Longarm said. "And you look good in that Stetson. It'll stand up to a hard rain where a straw hat would have disintegrated."

"I like it when you use big words," she said, stroking his leg. "Like 'disintegrated.' Most any man I ever met back in West Virginia would have just said a hat would fall apart."

Longarm closed his eyes. "Forgive me for asking, but I got the impression that both you and Nola had been with Boris."

"You mean like *we* have been together?"

"That's right."

"It's true," Ruby admitted. "We both had our hearts set on marryin' Boris. He was almost as handsome as you, Custis. And ever so sweet. He should never have come West and gotten killed. Boris wasn't real smart, and he should have stayed to home."

"He probably did it because he thought that he could help his people . . . just like you and Nola are hoping."

"That's right. Boris could have been a preacher, only he couldn't read nor write. But he was the handsomest fella . . . outside of yourself . . . that I ever laid eyes upon. Half the women in our country was in love with him, and the other half was either too old or too young to think about such matters."

Longarm could feel his eyelids growing heavier by the moment. "I think I'm going to take a little nap."

"You do that, Custis, darling. And when you wake up all rested, maybe we'll have us a little tumble in the leaves. Would you like that?"

"I sure would."

She patted him affectionately on the crotch and then said, "I'm going to go for a walk up the stream. Be back in a while."

"Watch out for timber rattlers," Longarm warned. "They're plentiful in these mountains."

"I'm a country girl, remember? I know how to take care of myself out in the woods."

"I'm sure you do," he said.

When Longarm awoke, he felt refreshed and ready to make love to Ruby. He looked around, but she was still out walking. Longarm yawned, stretched, and then climbed to his feet. He took out his pocket watch, and was surprised to see that he'd slept for several hours. It was getting late in the afternoon.

He walked over to their horses and tightened the cinches.

"Hey, Ruby," he called. "It's time we headed back to town."

There was no answer, so Longarm buckled on his six-gun and decided he'd go see if he could find that West Virginia girl. Most likely, she'd gotten engrossed in their new surroundings and had just forgotten the time. Longarm wasn't too worried because Ruby was strong and surely not the type to get turned around and lost in the heavy forest.

He followed the stream, looking for her and starting to grow anxious. "Ruby, where are you? Ruby!"

A branch snapped behind him and a gravelly voice ordered, "You can shut your big yap now, Custis Long. Put your hands up high and turn around *real* slow."

Longarm felt a river of dread pass down his spine, for he recognized the voice from his childhood and knew that the man who was behind him was Jude Haskill.

"I said put your hands up!"

Longarm heard the ominous cocking of a rifle's hammer.

"I ain't going to ask you again, Custis, and you know us Haskill boys never miss what we aim for." Longarm heard the haunting, insane laughter from his childhood. "Say, maybe I'll blow your knees out from under you first, then start working my way up to your spine."

There was nothing to do but turn around slowly and stare into Jude's cold, emotionless eyes one more time. "What did you do with Ruby?" Longarm asked.

"She's with my cousins and brothers. I wanted to face you by myself," Jude said. "I remember how you once caught me with a lucky punch; I have been waitin' for this chance to get even all these years."

Jude was even wilder-looking than expected. His teeth were either missing or stained by tobacco juice, and he bore the scars of some terrible knife fights and fistfights. Longarm knew he was looking at a cold-blooded killer who wouldn't hesitate to shoot him in the belly and laugh while he died in agony.

"Jude, I recall that we were just kids that took a strong dislike to each other back in the eastern hill country," Longarm said, his hands over his head, playing a desperate game for time. "There was nothing personal between us."

"Oh, the hell it warn't!" Jude spat a stream of tobacco juice onto the forest floor. He had turned out big, like all the men in his family, sharp-faced, with a long, sloping jaw and heavy brows. Shaggy black hair poked out from under his shapeless hat, and he had clothes that looked as filthy as those Longarm had discarded in Santa Fe.

"I'm a federal marshal," Longarm said, wondering if that would help or hurt his chances of surviving this encounter. "If you kill me, they'll come after you and never stop until you're either dead or sentenced to a life in prison."

Jude bayed with laughter. "I guess you know that we already killed Boris Bugabee." He patted his shirt. "Got his half of the Arizona treasure map too."

"That map is a hoax."

"A what?"

"A hoax. That means that map is a fake. I looked at it, and I've seen dozens of maps like that sold on the street corners of every big town in the West. There's no treasure in Arizona."

"You're dead wrong about that," Jude snarled. "The map was passed along by Honest Willard. And he ain't never lied to no one, not even a Haskill, in all his worthless years. He died, and now we got both halves of his map."

Longarm's heart sank. "You got Ruby's half."

"It ain't her half anymore. But don't fret. We figure she might know a few things that ain't on the map, so we're taking her along to Arizona with us. Sure nice of you to buy her all those nice new duds! She looks real fine, and we're gonna take special care of that girl."

He winked and it was obscene. "Yes, sir, we'll give her lots of real close and *personal* attention."

Jude laughed again, and it was all that Longarm could do not to yield to his hatred and either charge or go for his six-gun. But that, of course, was exactly what Jude wanted, and Longarm knew that he wouldn't stand a chance of winning.

"So where is Ruby right now?"

"Like I said, she's not far away."

"How many of you swine came West?"

"Swine?" Jude's eyes narrowed. "Is that what you called us?"

Longarm could feel his heart pounding harder. "Yes, but on second thought, I realize that calling you and your inbred brothers swine is an insult to pigs."

"Oh," Jude whispered, the rifle shaking in his clenched hands, "I'm gonna kill you real slow. And before I'm done, you're going to be begging me for mercy."

"Not likely."

"Reach down with your left hand and ease that gun out of your holster. Keep it butt to the front, and then drop it to the ground and move aside."

Longarm hesitated.

"Do as I say or I'll shoot!"

"All right." Longarm brought his left hand down and clasped the butt of his pistol. There was no way that he could snap the weapon around fast and fire at Jude.

"Easy, Marshal. Now drop it and step aside."

Longarm dropped the gun in the leaves knowing his only remaining chance was the hidden derringer attached to his watch fob. Fortunately, the double-barreled little .44 was still resting in his vest pocket.

"Now," Jude said, looking as if he were starting to really enjoy himself, "I want you to put your hands back over your head, turn around, and start walking straight up through the trees like your were before."

Longarm had no idea what the man had in mind, but every moment he lived was another moment he could think of some way out of this mess.

"Straight through the trees," Jude repeated, "and don't look back or do a damn thing but walk with your hands high over your head."

Longarm started walking and thinking about how he could possibly escape this man. The trees were fairly thick, and if he could just get one between himself and Jude, he'd have at least the slimmest of chances to draw his derringer and make a stand. Then, if Jude was angry and foolish enough to come barging in after him, Longarm just might be able to kill him with the derringer, whose accurate range was no better than fifty feet.

"Where are we going?"

"Just keep your mouth shut and your legs movin'."

Longarm did as he was told. He kept walking and watching and waiting for either a bullet in his back or a chance to leap for the safety of a pine. But he could hear Jude close behind him, and that cut down his odds of making a break.

"I hear that your pa whipped you even worse than I did after our fight," Longarm said. "I heard that your pa just didn't understand how you, being older and bigger, could let me beat you so bad."

"Shut up!"

"But I could have told your pa why I won and you got whipped. It was because you were always just a bully and you'd never fought anyone who hated you as much as I did."

"You got me with a lucky punch!"

"Oh, the hell you say," Longarm told the man behind him. "I was so filled with hatred for all the years you'd teased and bullied me that you could have had a club and I'd still have whipped you. And I could do it now one-handed."

"Ha! One-handed? Why, that'll be the day."

"Why don't you try me?" Longarm taunted. "Tie one of my hands to my belt and let's see who is left standing."

"Now why would I do that?"

"Because," Longarm said, "if you don't, you'll never know if I could beat you with one hand tied."

"You couldn't do it with *both* hands!"

"If you're so sure of that, why not take the chance? Or did I put a fear in you that never died?"

"Damn you!"

Longarm felt the barrel of Jude's rifle strike him in the back of his head. It was a stunning blow that knocked him flat on his face. He momentarily lost consciousness, and knew that Jude had opened his scalp to the bone. He might have stayed unconscious, but Jude kicked and then hauled him to his feet cussing and screaming oaths.

Longarm didn't remember much after that as they trudged through the woods. The blow to the back of his head had taken the spring out of his step, and it was all he could do to stay upright. He could feel a trickle of blood leaking down his neck to his shoulders and spine.

"Hey!" Jude shouted. "Look what I brought us!"

Longarm saw four Haskill men. Close by, they had Ruby tied to a tree, her blouse torn open at the front so that her breasts were exposed. Just the sight of her being so badly mistreated filled Longarm's stomach with bile; hot rage burned the fog from his mind.

"Look at the high-and-mighty United States Marshal Custis Long now," Jude crowed. "Ain't he a sorry sight!"

The four men laughed and came forward. One punched Longarm in the jaw, and when he staggered, another aimed a kick at his groin, but Longarm twisted and the blow caught him on the hip and sent him sprawling.

Longarm lay still for a moment, then climbed to his feet. "I told Jude I could whip him one-handed, but he's too much of a coward to take me on. He still thinks I got lucky when I beat him up as a boy . . . but I wasn't lucky . . . I was tougher. And I still am. He's scared to take the chance and fight using his two hands against my one."

Jude raised his rifle and took aim at Longarm's heart.

"No, please!" Ruby screamed.

Longarm thought Jude was going to kill him for sure, but instead, one of the brothers called, "It'd be fun to whip him, wouldn't it, Jude? Whip him to death and pay him back for what he once did to you."

"Yeah," Jude said, "I could beat him to death with my bare fists."

"Then do it!" another brother urged. "You always said that you wanted to fight him again."

"I *will* do it," Jude said, standing his rifle against a pine tree. "You boys will get a show for sure today."

Longarm knew he was in no condition to fight, so he argued for time.

"I was telling Jude that your Arizona treasure map is worthless. I've seen maps like that sold all over the West. One of the oldest con games is for some busted prospector to bring a map into a saloon and start talking about the rich mining claim he's just staked but can't work because he's broke. And pretty soon, some sucker will get the gold fever and the next thing . . . he'll be forking over money to the prospector for a share of the claim. And a map . . . just like Willard Bugabee's, will appear and the hook is set in the sucker's mouth."

Longarm took a deep breath or two and said, "Only, usually there's only one man stupid enough to fall for such a story. But in your case, it was *nine*."

The Haskill men exchanged glances. Jude frowned and said, "There's only five of us here . . . or maybe you forgot how to count."

"I killed Clem, Bobby, and Earl at a farmhouse just outside Denver about ten days ago," Longarm said, figuring the word would either win him a bullet or a fight to the death with Jude. "Oh, and it was your brother Ernie who led us to that farmhouse. I shot him to death too."

"Damn you!" one of the brothers screeched. "You killed 'em all?"

"That's right. But I did have the help of the Denver marshal and his deputies."

"I'm going to beat you to a pulp," Jude hissed, balling his fists and coming straight at Longarm. "And you can use both your damned hands."

Longarm's ears were ringing from the blow he'd already taken and his legs were unsteady as he waited for Jude to throw the first punch. When it came, Longarm ducked and swung, but missed and then paid the price. Jude hit him like the kick of a mule, and Longarm went crashing to the ground accompanied by the hoots and hollers of the Haskill men.

"Stomp him, Jude. Stomp the shit out of him!"

Longarm would have been stomped, but he managed to roll sideways, dodging kicks and trying to find a chance to regain his footing.

Jude was incredibly strong, and when Longarm did climb back on his feet, the man tackled him and they went rolling, punching, and gouging. Jude tried to get a thumb in Longarm's eye, but Longarm bit the thumb so hard that his teeth severed the thumb joint. Jude howled and smashed Longarm with his elbow nearly breaking his facial bones.

Longarm rolled and lashed out with his boot just as Jude came flying at him with both knees doubled and aimed for his chest. The boot caught Jude in the side of the face and when he landed, his knees buried themselves in the leaves. Longarm jumped around behind the man and got him in a headlock, then tried to snap his neck. But Jude rolled his shoulders and sent Longarm flying.

"Get him, Jude! Kill him!"

Longarm didn't get up fast enough, and Jude hammered him with an uppercut that nearly finished the fight. Longarm fell back and kicked Jude in the stomach. The man grunted and Longarm kicked again, this time aiming for Jude's right knee and connecting. Jude cried out and his knee buckled. Longarm was on him in a flash, driving his fists into the man's body and face, and then spinning their bodies around so that he could use the dazed and bloodied Jude as a shield against the other Haskill men.

"Let him go!" one of them yelled, his gun in his fist.

Longarm fumbled in his vest for his derringer, and when it came out he placed the barrel against Jude's skull.

"Drop your guns or I'll blow his brains out!" Longarm cried.

Jude struggled mightily, but Longarm's forearm was locked around his throat and the derringer was pressed hard into the man's ear. "Drop it or I'll kill him."

"You do that and you'll die."

"I will anyway."

"It's a standoff," one of the brothers said. "A damned standoff!"

Longarm was running on steam. He glanced over at Ruby, and during the instant their eyes connected, he saw hope.

"I'll let Jude go if you let the girl go," he said. "You got her map now."

"We ain't lettin' no one go!" a Haskill man cried, dragging out his gun and taking aim at Longarm and Jude.

"Hold it!" another of them shouted. "Let's think this thing out before we let him shoot Jude in the head."

For a few tense moments, no one said a word. Jude was gagging, and Longarm didn't dare let up the pressure of his choke hold. Finally, one of the Haskill men said, "All right. The girl for Jude."

"Untie her," Longarm ordered, "and let her run back for our horses."

"If we do that, how we gonna know you still won't shoot our brother?"

"Because," Longarm said, "I'm no fool and I also want to get out of this alive."

All of them had their guns or rifles pointed at Longarm, but he kept his head down low and they were afraid of hitting Jude by mistake.

"Untie Ruby," one of them said at last.

Longarm risked a glance at her and yelled, "Head for our horses!"

"I'm not leaving you like this!"

"Go!" Longarm ordered.

Ruby shook her head. "If I leave you now I'll never see you alive again. Custis, we go together or not at all."

One of the Haskill men swore something about women, but Longarm's mind was racing and he knew Ruby's mind couldn't be changed. "All right. Go get the horses and bring them back here. We'll ride out with Jude."

"No, you aren't," the Haskill man swore. "Not alive you aren't."

"We'll drop him off and then you all head for Arizona with the Picacho Peak treasure map. We've got nothing to stop you and no map. It's the only way that Jude is getting out of this alive. I've got nothing to lose and I'm not bluffing."

"All right, Ruby. Go get your horses and come back. If you don't, ain't God himself could save Custis."

Ruby shot Longarm a glance, and then took off running as if her legs were on fire. They waited, hearing her crashing through the forest. She was back in less than fifteen minutes, and not one word had passed between Longarm and the Haskill men who so desperately wanted to see him dead.

Longarm said. "If nobody does anything stupid, then nobody dies. Ruby, lead off back toward town. Jude and I will follow along. We get a mile without these boys trying to kill me, then Jude goes free."

"How do we know that you won't kill our brother anyway?"

"Why should I do something like that?" Longarm asked. "I just whipped him again, didn't I?"

It was a crazy thing to say, but it caught the Haskill men off guard, and before any of them could figure it out, Longarm was backing Jude away, and then they were hurrying after Ruby into the trees.

Longarm dropped Jude when he couldn't support the

half-conscious man any longer. He bent down and said, "I'd kill you right now except that your brothers would probably catch Ruby and kill us both. So I'm turning you free, but we'll meet again in Arizona and I'll finish you off once and for all."

Jude was still swearing when Longarm and Ruby raced their horses for Santa Fe. They both knew they were lucky to still be alive.

Chapter 10

It was dusk when Longarm and Ruby rode back into Santa Fe. They were both in rough shape, especially Longarm, who kept seeing double and having spells of intense dizziness. Ruby wasn't doing very well either, and Longarm didn't have the heart to ask her what the Haskill men had done to her either before or during the time she'd been tied to a tree.

"We're going after them tomorrow," Longarm said. "They might think we've given up or been scared off, but by Gawd we *are* going after them."

"There are five Haskill men against just the pair of us," Ruby said. "I'm not sure we'd have much of a chance even if we did catch them."

"We'll catch them," Longarm vowed, hanging onto his saddlehorn and trying to keep the world from spinning too fast.

"You don't look to be in any shape to travel in the morning," Ruby told him. "How's your head?"

"Not good." He closed one eye and the double vision remained. "Keep that blouse pulled together or you're going to give the boys a real eyeful."

"They ripped the buttons and everything underneath

113

away," she said, her voice sounding old. "They pinched and licked and . . ."

"I'm sorry," Longarm said. "I should never have let you out of my sight. It was just pure bad luck that they happened to find us out there by that stream."

"It didn't work that way," Ruby said. "They spotted us in Santa Fe and then waited until we left on our picnic this morning. They trailed us out of town and then caught us off guard."

"That won't happen a second time," Longarm vowed.

"Here's the livery," Ruby said, reining in her horse.

But Longarm didn't make a move to dismount. "I don't think I'm up to the walk back to our place," he admitted. "I'd better stay in the saddle. We can pay one of Juan's kids to lead the horses back here."

Ruby nodded because she could see that Longarm was struggling just to stay seated. "Custis, I think maybe we ought to find a doctor before we go back to our room."

"I'll be fine," he promised. "I just need to lie down for a while. Maybe have a glass of whiskey and a bite to eat. Tomorrow, I'll be ready to ride. Can't afford to let Jude and his boys get too far ahead."

But when they rode up to the hitching rail in front of the Escobar place and Longarm tried to dismount, he became so dizzy that he toppled to the ground enveloped in a swirling cloud of darkness.

That was the last thing he remembered.

It was two days later when he regained consciousness. A man he guessed was a doctor was staring into his eyeball with a thumb pressed up against his eyelid. Longarm blinked and his eyelid snapped shut, then snapped open again.

"Well, Marshal Long, good to have you back among us again," the doctor said with much too much cheeriness. "You've taken quite a long nap."

Longarm sat upright, but a bolt of lightning struck the middle of his cracked skull and he had to lie back down again. "Ohhh," he groaned. "It feels like someone ran over my head with a train."

"You've got a bad concussion, young man. You're fortunate to be among the living after taking a blow like that to the back of your head. You must have a cranium as thick as a coconut shell."

Longarm had never even seen a coconut, but he guess they were very thick.

"Are you still seeing double?" the doctor asked.

Longarm wanted to say no, but there were two identical doctors and two Rubys. He closed one eye, and the doubles swam in and out of each other.

"Not fair," the doctor said. "You can't go around with one eye squeezed shut."

"I don't feel too good in the belly either," he admitted.

"Do you feel nauseated?"

"You mean sick?"

"Yes, that's what I mean." Longarm nodded his head, and that was a mistake.

"Yes," the doctor said, "those are common symptoms of a concussion, and yours happens to be one of the worst I've seen in quite a few years. Like I said, you are fortunate to be among the living."

"Well," Longarm told the man, "I need to get up and get after the Haskill men before they get completely out of New Mexico."

"You're not going anywhere for a month," the man said without equivocation.

"A month!"

"You heard me."

Longarm took a deep breath and jutted his jaw. "I'll give myself a couple of days at the most."

"If you try to do too much too soon, you'll only set

115

yourself back and possibly incur some long-term brain injury. Is that what you want?"

"Of course not, but I've a job to do."

"Your job right now is to rest and recover," the doctor assured Longarm. "And I don't want you to get out of the bed even for bowel movements."

"What?"

"You'll have to use a bedpan."

"You're out of your mind, Doc! I'm not doin' it."

"Suit yourself and pay the consequences. Miss Bugabee here warned me that you were obstinate and unreasonably stubborn. She wasn't exaggerating."

Longarm watched the man close up his medical bag and prepare to take his leave. "Doc?"

"Yeah?"

"What about headache powders?"

"I've already left you a good supply with Miss Bugabee."

"Cigars and whiskey?"

"Out of the question!"

"Come on, Doc! It's bad enough just staying here, but now you're taking away all my pleasures."

"Not all of them," Ruby corrected.

Longarm looked at her and saw the woman wink. He knew what Ruby meant, and he was grateful that she seemed to have made a complete recovery from her own harrowing ordeal at the hands of the Haskill men.

"Good day," the doctor said. "I'll return tomorrow morning to see how you are progressing."

"I'll be fine by then."

"Ha!" the man barked as he strode out the door.

Longarm waited until they were alone and then he said, "You look pretty fit, Ruby. Are you all right?"

"I have to be now for the both of us. Besides, they didn't have time to do what they intended to me. If you

116

hadn't showed up, I was going to try and kill one of them and then myself."

"Maybe you ought to return to Denver and stay with Nola," Longarm told the woman. "You've been through enough already."

"So have you, but you're not quitting."

"That's because it's my job to rid the West of people like Jude Haskill and his brothers. It isn't your job."

"You need me. You need to wire Denver and see if you can get some reinforcements. I don't think we can tangle with them again and count on being so lucky."

"It wasn't just luck, Ruby. I consciously goaded Jude into a fight knowing that if I could get his body between myself and his brothers, I had a good chance of surviving. And if I could survive, I knew that you could survive."

Ruby sat down on the edge of his bed. "I was so scared I peed myself while I was roped to that tree." Her chin quivered. "I was mad and ashamed and feeling like I was already dead."

He took her hand. "You did just fine. You collected our horses, and we couldn't have gotten out of there without them."

Longarm could feel Ruby trembling, and he pulled her down on top of him and held her tight. "Think about returning to Denver while I push on to Arizona."

"I couldn't do that."

"Sure you could, and besides, I work best alone."

"Custis, I made a promise to the poor people back home that we'd find that treasure and use the money to help all of them. If I didn't do everything I could out here, I don't believe I could face those trusting folks. Besides, Boris died trying to help 'em, and I've got to try to help 'em too."

"I understand that, but this isn't what you've been trained to do," Longarm argued. "Those Haskill men are animals. If I go down, I'm dead. But if you go down,

117

you'll end up at their mercy praying for a quick death. There's a big difference, Ruby."

She didn't say anything, and Longarm held her quietly the rest of the morning. He'd said his piece, and he wished she'd go back to Denver, but he couldn't make her do his bidding.

Longarm was on his feet the next day, but too dizzy and sick to do much more than avoid the use of a bedpan. He sat by the window and watched Ruby out in the patio garden talking to Juan and his family. He heard Ruby laugh, and knew that she would soon be her former, indomitable self, but they both needed time to recover.

After three more days, however, Longarm couldn't stand waiting any longer, and was ready to leave Santa Fe. "Doc," he said, fully dressed and wearing his holster and gun on his left hip, "I've got to be on my way."

"You aren't nearly ready yet."

"I'll be fine. I wish you'd talk Ruby into either staying here in Santa Fe or else returning to Denver."

"I've nothing to do with that," he said dismissively. "I'm a doctor and I deal in terms of the human body. Ruby's body looks fine."

"Yes," Longarm said, "it does."

Ruby gave them both a look that could have killed.

"Marshal Long," the doctor said, "are you having any more double vision?"

"No."

"Headaches?"

"All gone."

"When you sit up do you get dizzy?"

"Nope."

"Then I guess I can't order you to stay," the doctor told him. "But it's clear that you are underweight and in need of some rest."

"I've been resting for almost two weeks! Doctor, I need to get started for Arizona."

"Not on a horse," the man insisted. "You can take a train or a stagecoach, but no horseback riding for at least a couple of weeks."

"All right."

"You promise?" the doctor asked. "Because the jarring ride of a horse would really be unwise."

"I promise."

"Then go and Godspeed."

There was a stagecoach bound for Albuquerque, then continuing down to Socorro, and Longarm meant to be on it the next morning. He would have to sell his horse and saddle, but he wasn't attached to either and both were easy to replace. When he told Ruby of his intentions, she insisted on selling her own mount and saddle as well.

"You can't do that," Longarm told her. "The horse and saddle you're using belong to Marshal Leland. He probably expects them back."

"I'll send him a telegram and ask," Ruby replied.

The telegram came back within hours, and the news was that Marshal Ben Leland didn't care much about his horse and he gave Ruby full permission to sell it and his saddle, provided she got at least fifty dollars for the pair. But the really shocking news was that he had asked Nola to marry him. She'd consented, and the marriage would take place as soon as Longarm and Ruby returned from Arizona.

"Can you believe this good news!" Ruby cried, waving the telegram in front of Longarm's face. "My sister is gonna get hitched to a real Western marshal and live in Denver, Colorado!"

"That's really good news," Longarm said. "But I'll bet that you'll miss her when you go back to West Virginia."

Ruby's smile faded. "You're right. Nola and I have

been so close all these years. But I'm still very happy for her."

"Why don't you go back to Denver and help her plan the wedding?"

"No," Ruby insisted. "I talked you into helping us with this Picacho Peak business, and I'm not letting you go on alone. Tomorrow when the stagecoach leaves for Socorro, I'll be sitting at your side."

Longarm knew that he could not change her mind, so he wasted no more time in trying.

"How far is it from Socorro to Picacho?" Ruby asked.

"It's still a long way, but we can get on the Southern Pacific Railroad, which will take us all the way to Tucson, and then rent a pair of horses that will carry us up to where this supposed treasure is to be found."

"Sounds good," she said.

Longarm didn't want to tell Ruby that they'd soon be entering the desert and, in late August, it could be a living hell. Ruby might think that she knew what heat was, but she really had no idea.

That, unfortunately, was just about to change.

Chapter 11

Their trip to Tucson had been long, dusty, and blazing hot. When Longarm and Ruby got off the train they were perspiring heavily, and wasted no time in heading for the nearest porch where they could rest in the shade.

Ruby looked at the hot Southwestern town and shook her head in amazement. "Why on earth would *anyone* want to live here?"

"Tucson has a perfect winter climate," Longarm replied. "And a rich history. Until recently, it was the territorial capital of Arizona. Long before that, it was the center of Spanish colonization and trade, but back in those early times the town was always under siege by the Apache. And in fact, Geronimo and various bands of the Chiricahua Apache are still raising hell in this part of the country."

"Our government should have let the Apache have this part of the country as long as the sun shines by day and the moon shines at night," Ruby said. "Why we wanted this part of Arizona it is way beyond me."

Longarm removed his hat and wiped his brow with a handkerchief. "A lot of wealthy Eastern people travel out here to stay during the winters for their health. Tucson has a good water supply from the Santa Cruz River and its wells. Farmers are arriving every day because crops of all kinds flourish here, and I expect that this town will keep growing, thanks to the railroad and agriculture. Also, Tombstone and Bisbee are big mining towns, and there are gold and silver to be found in the mountains you see surrounding us in the distance."

Longarm could sense that Ruby remained unimpressed, and she proved it when she said, "The population here in Tucson may be growing, but it's also growing in hell. And quite honestly, I'd bet anything that they are both about the same temperature."

"It won't be any cooler where we're headed next," Longarm warned. "Let's find a room for the night, a good meal, and rest. Tomorrow we'll figure out how we're going to get up to Picacho Peak."

"What about that bank business that you are supposed to look into down here for your boss?"

"I'll do that when we return," Longarm said. "The important thing right now is to get to Picacho Peak."

"Do you think Jude and the rest have already gotten that far?"

"I don't know," Longarm said with a shrug of his broad shoulders. "It's possible."

"If they've already gotten that treasure and left, I'll just die!"

"You might die anyway," Longarm told her, suddenly very serious. "This is your last chance to show good sense and stay behind and out of danger."

"Not me," she told him. "We're in this together all the way."

Longarm appreciated that sentiment even if it was badly misguided.

That evening while Ruby was taking a bath, Longarm went down to have a few beers at a saloon called the Calico Cat. It was there that he met a man named Travis

Oates who owned a small freighting company that hauled goods back and forth between Phoenix and Tucson.

"So you always pass right by Picacho Peak."

"Oh, sure," the man said. "That's where we stop for the night to rest our mules. There's a trading post there, along with a saloon and little hotel. It's pretty quiet there in the summertime what with this heat. Nobody but a fool or a working man like myself is going to be on that road at this time of the year unless they absolutely have no choice."

Longarm had earlier sent a long telegram to Billy Vail in Denver explaining how he'd gotten a concussion and how he and Ruby were about to depart for Picacho Peak. He'd promised that, when this Haskill business was over, he would return to Tucson and investigate the banking situation. He also said that he was almost out of funds and could use an additional hundred dollars.

Now, as Travis Oates talked, it occurred to Longarm that he just might be able to get a ride up to Picacho without having the expense of renting horses and outfits.

"What would you charge for me and my lady friend to go along with you up to Picacho tomorrow?" Longarm asked.

"Now why would you want to go up there with a lady?"

"It's a long story that has to do with the last battle fought out West between the Union and Confederacy," Longarm said. "And one of the Union soldiers who claimed he buried a cache of gold close to the peak."

"Well," Oates said, "there are a million-and-one treasure stories. Most of them take place over in the Superstition Mountains, but just about anyplace you go in Arizona you'll have someone trying to sell you a treasure map."

"I know that," Longarm said, "but the lady I'm traveling with is sure that this one has some basis of fact. It's one of those deals where you have to go and find out for yourself."

Longarm didn't see any point in telling this man about Jude Haskill and his brothers and cousins killing Boris and nearly killing himself and the Bugabee sisters. It was too complicated, and besides, Longarm never had been one who thought it wise to tell strangers his business. He hadn't even told the freight company owner that he was a federal marshal because that was none of the freighter's business.

"We're low on funds and could use a ride up there," Longarm told the man. "How much?"

"You and your woman can ride along for free," Oates said. "I'm hauling a couple of tons of grain up to Phoenix. We'll be taking four wagons up and it's a two-day trip. Stop tomorrow night in Picacho, and get to Phoenix the day after tomorrow. Then I'll hunt around for a load in Phoenix to bring back down to Tucson. If I'm lucky, I'll return early next week."

"I hope we can find the treasure or at least take care of all our business before then," Longarm said, "but if not, we'd need a ride back down here and could come with you."

"That would suit me fine," Oates said. "We've had Apache troubles on this run, and if you can use that six-gun on your hip, you'd be a welcome addition. The more guns we have to fight off Apache or anyone else that wants to ambush us and take our wagons and stock . . . the better."

Longarm thought the arrangement sounded good all the way around. He bought Oates another whiskey, and promised the man that he and Ruby would be ready to leave Tucson by five o'clock the next morning.

"We need to get out that early so we can get to Picacho by mid-afternoon," the freight company owner explained.

"If you don't quit by mid-afternoon, you're risking your mules and drivers to heat stroke."

"Are you pretty sure that my lady friend and I can get a room at the hotel?" Longarm asked.

"No question about that. Now, like I said, if it were midwinter, there might be a problem."

"Sounds good."

Longarm returned to his room, and the bath was still warm, so he crawled in with Ruby, who was taking her good sweet time soaking up this rare luxury.

"I put some bath oil in the water, so you're going to smell real sweet tonight," Ruby said as she reached out and fondled his manhood.

"If you keep doing that," Longarm told her, "we won't be waiting until tonight."

"Oh, really?"

Longarm saw that look in her eyes that he had learned to mean that Ruby wanted to have a romp. And since he'd just gotten into the tub, he motioned for her to come on over and mount up. Ruby was only too happy to oblige, and then they started humping and splashing, until the floor was covered with water and they were grasping and gasping with the hot fire of their sloppy but energetic union.

When it was over, Longarm reached for the soap and asked Ruby to scrub his back. Afterward, he returned the favor, although he also added a chest scrub that got Ruby excited and initiated them into another session of wild coupling and splashing.

"Some bath," Ruby said later as she crawled out of the tub and reached for her clothes. "Now I feel clean and completely satisfied."

"Me too," Longarm said from the tub. "How about lighting us up a cigar?"

Ruby lit the cigar, and Longarm smoked it down enjoying the sensations of smoke and water.

"We ought to celebrate tonight," Ruby said.

"We'll do it when we come back from Picacho and this Haskill business is finished," Longarm told her. "And by the way, we're leaving at five o'clock tomorrow morning."

"Five o'clock!"

"You can stay behind if you want," Longarm said, explaining the travel arrangement he had made for them early the next morning. He ended by saying, "I've sent a telegram asking for more expense money, but we can't wait for that to happen and this saves us a lot of money."

"Yeah, I suppose so."

"You don't look too excited."

"I'm not," Ruby answered. "How are we supposed to search on foot for either the treasure or the Haskills?"

"Good question," Longarm replied. "We'll think on it when we get to Picacho."

"I can't believe I'm finally going to be there," Ruby mused out loud. "After all this time coming West and with everything that has happened to us and to Nola and poor Boris, it seems strange. Until now, Picacho has always just been a name . . . like a fairytale . . . that we were trying to reach but wondered if it even existed."

"It exists, but it's hardly a fairy tale," Longarm said. "The peak stands alone and it is impressive. It's black and volcanic and rises right out of the desert floor so that it can be seen for miles and miles. There are ocotillo and huge specimens of the many-armed saguaro cactus dotting its sides, and you'll find that it has wild pigs and burros that come down off its slopes at night to drink from several springs at its base."

"I wish we were going up there in wintertime," Ruby told him. "I have a feeling that it won't be nearly as attractive a place tomorrow in the heat."

"We didn't come here for a vacation," Longarm reminded her. "We came to see if we could find that Spanish gold that Uncle Honest Willard Bugabee was supposed to have buried. That, and to settle the score with the Haskill men for what they did to Boris and your sister."

"I know. Any chance that we could ask the local marshal to come along with a few of his deputies?"

"I already stopped by to visit and make that suggestion. The marshal of Tucson explained that he is hired by the Tucson city council and he'd risk getting fired by them if he left he city unprotected. Sorry, Ruby, but it's just you and me."

"But we do have the element of surprise. Right?"

"I hope so," Longarm said. "Because quite frankly, that would be all that we have in our favor."

They left the next morning at five, and there wasn't much conversation. Just a quick introduction of Ruby to Oates, and then a few terse orders to the mule skinners as they made their final, hurried preparations to roll out of Tucson in the dark.

Travis Oates said, "You two can sit on the seat beside me or stretch out on that pile of grain and sleep until the sun comes up."

"We'll sleep," Ruby told him without a second of hesitation.

"You sleep," Longarm told her. "I'll keep Travis company."

So the heavily laden freight wagons creaked out of town, and an hour or so later, Longarm had the joy of watching the sun come up over the eastern mountains. There was, he knew, something especially beautiful about an Arizona sunrise. Maybe it was that the punished land was so hushed and still during a desert dawn. Or because of shimmering heat waves that radiated off the desert's floor, or the special clarity of the air. It could have been all of those things, but Longarm figured it was because the rocks and cactus that jutted from this earth gave one the feeling that they were beings beseeching God for one more moment of coolness before the daily struggle to survive began anew.

"Ain't it something, though?" Oates whispered as they stared at the rising sun and watched the high, wispy clouds turn salmon and gold. "When I see the saguaro at dawn, they remind me of ancient giants standing guard over this entire desert."

"I've had that same feeling," Longarm admitted. "And you don't get it anyplace but in the Arizona desert."

"Maybe the sunrises and sunsets out here are so spectacular because the land is so ugly," Oates mused. "I don't know, but there are times when even the desert takes on a beauty of its own."

"I agree. I'm from Colorado, and there's nothing to compare to the Rocky Mountains, but I've learned that the desert can also be beautiful. Because I grew up in West Virginia, I came West thinking that no land was worth looking at unless it was covered with trees and green bushes."

"I know what you mean," Oates said, "because I came from Pennsylvania and felt exactly the same way for a few years."

"Why did you leave the East?"

"Same as most of us. The war was coming on and my father was in poor health. He had bad lungs from smoking tobacco for too many years, and the doctor told us he'd live longer in Arizona."

"Did he?"

"Yep. My father lived to be sixty-eight, and he wouldn't have lasted past sixty if we'd stayed in Pennsylvania. But I sure hated this country when we first arrived. We were almost killed twenty miles east of Tucson by Cochise and his Apache. Would have been if a cavalry patrol hadn't chanced upon us. We all put up a hell of a fight and drove Cochise off, but not before we lost ten men and three women. All I wanted to do was to go back to Pennsylvania."

"How old were you?"

"Twenty-two. Now, I'm glad I stuck, and I'm doing well. Have a wife and five children in Tucson, and I hope to build this business up and hand it over to them . . . if they want it."

Longarm and the freighter talked on for a while as the sun lifted off the horizon and then the earth began to grow hot. Longarm knew that by eight o'clock, the temperature would be pushing into the low nineties, and by ten o'clock, it might top one hundred degrees.

"How do your mules handle this extreme heat?"

"Ordinarily, they do fine, but this heat is too much even for mules. Did you know that the United States Army once brought camels over from the Far East and experimented with using them to haul supplies across the deserts of the Southwest?"

"I'd heard pieces of that story and always wondered if it was fact or fiction."

"It's true," Oates assured him. "They brought about seventy-five camels over in 1855 when Jefferson Davis was the Secretary of War. The idea was to use them in pack trains hauling United States Army supplies to the various forts down in this country. They even brought experienced camel riders over, but the whole thing failed."

"Why?"

"Lots of reasons," Oates said. "Mostly, though, everyone hated the damned ugly beasts. They'd spit on the Americans, who quickly learned camels have a foul disposition. And when the camel trains came upon horses or mules, why, the horses and mules would take one look at those camels and then spook and go crazy. There are stories that I've heard where entire wagon trains were wrecked because of the camels."

"Whatever happened to the camels?" Longarm asked.

"Did the Army ship them back to the Far East?"

"Nope. They just turned them loose in the deserts."

"I've never seen a wild camel out here."

"A few still exist," Oates assured him. "I've seen a couple running loose, but most of them have been shot by prospectors just out of meanness or for their meat."

"I can't imagine eating some mangy camel's meat."

"I've heard it tastes like dung," Oates said. "Wouldn't surprise me that the meat is as foul-tasting as their dispositions."

"Me neither," Longarm said, trying to imagine what a camel train would look like crossing this desolate country.

"There it is," Oates said much, much later that day as he raised his finger to point straight north. "That's Picacho Peak."

Ruby climbed out of the wagon bed, dusting herself off and taking a seat between Longarm and the driver, who asked, "Did you catch a few winks of sleep, miss?"

"Yes, I did," she told the man, "but it got so hot back there that I woke up sweating."

"*Everything* sweats in this country," Oates said. "What do you think of Picacho Peak?"

Ruby squinted into the heat and studied the towering rocky landmark. "It's even bigger than I'd expected."

"It's huge, all right," Oates agreed.

Ruby shook her head. "But I can't for the life of me imagine why my uncle and his soldier friends would want to fight over such a barren piece of rock."

Longarm had to smile. "They weren't fighting over the peak itself, Ruby. They were fighting for control of the Arizona Territory, which they correctly figured had a lot of gold, silver, and copper. All valuable to the war effort."

"Hell of a sorry place for good men to die," Ruby opined.

Both men laughed.

Ruby soon learned that distances were deceiving in the desert. It took them another two hours to reach the isolated settlement nestled at the base of the peak, and when they did, Longarm and Ruby hurried inside the combination saloon and hotel.

"Me and the lady need a room and a bath," Longarm said to the bartender. "And a bottle of your best whiskey."

"I can give you two out of the three," the man said. "Whiskey and a room. But no bath because we're short on water."

"I thought the springs at the base of the peak were reliable."

"Nope," the bartender told Longarm. "Some especially dry years they dwindle down to a trickle or even go dry. This is one of the drought years, so the only water we use here is what we drink. Mostly, we drink whiskey and beer."

Longarm had studied the little settlement closely during those last few hard, hot miles, and he could not see a black mule with a spot on its side or any other hard-used saddle horses indicating the presence of Jude Haskill and his bunch. That was both good and bad news. Good because it meant that he and Ruby would have some time to prepare a battle plan . . . bad because it might mean that Jude and his family might have already come, found the gold, and departed.

"Bartender," Longarm said as he paid for their room. "Have you had any visitors from West Virginia in the last week?"

"Nope. At least," the man added as he handed Longarm a bottle and two glasses, "I don't think so. You see, mister, it ain't considered smart in my business to ask customers where they came from or where they're headed."

"I understand, but these were all tall, scarred, and ugly men. Black hair and bad teeth. There were five of them, and they were as hard a bunch of critters as you'll ever have walk through your door."

"I ain't seen 'em, although there are some pretty rough men that pass this way. I've seen about the worst sorts as you can imagine."

"No, you haven't," Longarm said. "Not until you've seen the Haskill men."

Longarm took Ruby and the bottle to their cramped hotel room. It wasn't nice and it wasn't clean. Dust covered the sparse furniture, and when he whacked the bedspread, the dust billowed up in his face.

"It's not very nice here and it must be a hundred in this room," Ruby complained.

"We have no choice but to stay and sweat it out until the Haskill men show up looking for your uncle's gold."

"I almost hope they come soon."

Longarm threw his travel bag on the floor and removed his gunbelt, pants, and shirt. He stretched out on the bed and said, "Ruby, you insisted on coming, and we might as well take a nap. When the sun goes down it will cool off a little, but not much. We'll go eat and socialize. That's how our day will go until Jude and that bunch arrive."

"Won't the bartender and people wonder why we're staying in this hell hole?"

"They will, but they won't ask, and we won't answer any questions. We'll also start planning how we're going to face the Haskill bunch. One thing for sure, we can't take all of them on at the same time."

"I should expect not."

"So we'll have to divide and conquer," Longarm said as he closed his eyes, feeling the sweat popping from every pore of his body. "Divide and conquer is our only hope for success."

Ruby nodded and undressed. She stretched out on the

bed beside Longarm, but it was so suffocating in the room that neither of them thought about anything but how they could divide, conquer, find the gold, and then get the hell out of this blazing-hot Arizona desert.

Chapter 12

Longarm awoke early the next morning while Ruby continued to sleep. He quietly dressed in the predawn light, then headed over to the saloon, which also served as a kitchen and dining area. He was not surprised to see that Travis Oates and his three mule skinners were already eating and drinking their second cups of coffee.

"It's going to be a hot one out there today," Oates said. "But we ought to be in Phoenix by two o'clock, barring a breakdown."

"And that happens?"

"Oh, sure. As you know from yesterday, the road is full of potholes, and given the amount of weight we are carrying in those four wagons, it's easy to break an axle."

"Then what do you do?"

"Not much we can do except leave the broken wagon behind and continue on to Phoenix. Last time it happened, it took two days for a blacksmith to fix a busted axle and it cost me a small fortune. I lost time and money on that trip. But it happens, and you have to be prepared for anything."

"It sounds like a tough business," Longarm said.

"It is a tough business, but it's the only one that I know.

Before too many more years pass, a railroad will lay tracks between Phoenix and Tucson and I'll be out of business. I've got to make hay while the sun shines."

"It always shines in Arizona," Longarm said, sitting down beside the man and pouring a strong cup of coffee from a big pot.

Oates was wolfing down his breakfast, anxious to be on the road, and his teamsters were just as eager, knowing how the last few hours of the journey north would be punishing.

"We've got to get the teams hitched and be on our way," the freight operator said. "We'll see you on the way back in a few days ... week at the most depending if I get lucky and get a cargo needing to go south."

Longarm went to the door of the saloon with a steaming cup of coffee in his hand. A coyote howled somewhere out in the desert, sad and lonesome. Longarm figured the poor animal could hardly have picked a worse spot in the world to try and make its living.

The sunrise was brilliant as always, and before it faded, Oates and his wagons were rolling north.

The bartender, who also was the owner of the saloon, came to stand by Longarm in the doorway and watch the sunrise and departing wagons. "It's beautiful to see that sun come up, but we all know we're gonna pay for the pleasure."

"Yeah."

"Kind of like beautiful women, if you ask me."

Longarm hadn't a clue as to what the man was talking about, and it must have shown on his face because the bartender said, "What I meant was that this beautiful sunrise is soon gonna be gone and it's going to be hotter than hell. To my way of thinking, it's the same with beautiful women ... they bring you joy and make your heart swell, but all too quickly they're gone and leave you worse off than before you saw them."

"Sounds like you've had some bad luck with the women."

"I have," the bartender said as they watched the freight wagons top a low rise and then disappear as if the desert had swallowed them up whole. "So now I stay away from all but the old and ugly ones. That way, if they decide to leave you, so what?"

Longarm drained his coffee cup and headed back inside for a refill and his breakfast. *Some men,* he thought, *say the damnedest things.*

It was about ten o'clock that same morning when a horseman came galloping down the road toward Picacho from the north. Everyone was sitting in the saloon still sipping coffee and trying to ignore the rising heat when the rider let out a wild yell.

"Would you look at that fool," a man standing in the doorway said. "Running his horse like that in this awful heat. He'll kill his horse for sure if he keeps that pace up."

Longarm couldn't have agreed more as he and Ruby stepped out in the yard. Even though the rider was still at least a half mile away, everyone could see that his horse was covered with froth and foam from being ridden too hard in too much heat. And then, just as the horse drew nearer, they saw that it wasn't a horse at all but a mule and that its rider was Travis Oates.

"Something bad has happened," Longarm said, running up the road along with several of the other men.

The mule stopped when it saw the approaching men. It was out of wind, and it just quit running in the middle of the road and began to bray.

Longarm had always been a fine runner, and he was the first one from the saloon crowd to reach Oates, who had been shot in the chest and who was almost ready to pass out from loss of blood.

"What happened?" Longarm demanded, kneeling down beside the man and tearing open his shirt to try and staunch the flow of blood.

"We got ambushed," Oates gasped. "About ten miles up the road we caught heavy fire from rocks. I think it was Apache. All my men went down in the first volley, and when I saw they couldn't be helped, I got on my best mule and lit out of there as fast as I could. They shot at us, but that mule is faster than most horses and I got away."

Longarm glanced at the other men who had left the saloon and come to help. "Let's get him inside and see if we can get him patched up before he bleeds to death."

Ruby was waiting with a pail of clean water, and when they washed away the blood and dirt from the bullet wound, Longarm heaved a sigh of relief. "The bullet ricocheted off his ribs. Lots of blood loss, but it didn't tear up anything important."

"You mean I'm going to make it?" Oates whispered, pale but looking much relieved by this good news.

"That's right," Longarm told him. "Ruby can take care of you while I and a few volunteers go see if any of your men or mules are still alive."

"My mule skinners are all dead," Oates sobbed, tears filling his eyes. "I made sure of that before I left. The Apache must have been after the mules because they sure wouldn't have wanted the grain in our wagons."

"The Apache were after your mules, harness, and whatever else they could get from the dead bodies," the bartender said bitterly. "Was it that bastard Geronimo?"

Oates rolled his head back and forth on the bar where he'd been laid out. "I don't know. It happened so fast and there were so many shots fired that I didn't have time to do nothing but check my men. Bullets were flying all around me, and I knew I had to get the hell out of there or I'd be cut to pieces."

Longarm looked to Ruby. "Keep pressing that bandage down hard on his side until the bleeding stops, and then bind him up tight. It's a good thing that the bullet exited, or we'd have to dig it out."

"Do we have any medicine?"

The bartender said, "I've got nothin' but whiskey to use as disinfectant."

"Use it," Longarm said. "It'll burn like fire but it will help." He turned to the men who were standing around cursing Geronimo and his Apache, then asked for volunteers.

"I'll go," a huge humpbacked man who looked like he could whip a grizzly offered.

"Me too," another said.

Longarm got a third volunteer, and after they saddled horses, they rode north at a steady trot because it was getting hotter by the minute. Longarm and his posse were all heavily armed and good fighters, but he knew that they were still shorthanded if they ran into a large force of raiding Apache. Still, they had to go find out if there were any survivors.

When they topped a rise, they saw the wagons way off in the distance with four or five black turkey vultures already circling low overhead.

"It doesn't look too good," Longarm observed. "When we get closer, I want every man to fan out so we're not a bunched target. Keep your eyes wide open for the Apache. There are only four of us, and they might just decide that they still haven't finished today's bloody business."

"I can see one body," a rider said. "And he ain't moving."

"I see another," Longarm told his men. "I expect they never knew what hit them."

"The wagons and the grain look okay," a man said. "But there's no sign of Travis's mules."

"Apache like mule meat."

"Yeah, I know. They also like scalps."

As they trotted up the road toward Phoenix, Longarm knew they were easy targets for another ambush. There was a lot of cover on both sides of the road where Apache could hide and wait for just the right opportunity to open fire.

"Be alert," he warned as they drew closer to the abandoned wagons. "If the Apache are still here lying in wait, it'll be nearly impossible to see them until they start firing."

Longarm could feel sweat trickle down his spine, and he gripped his rifle tightly, eyes squinted as they tried to see everything on both sides of the road.

"Spread out," he ordered.

They separated and continued forward with Longarm the only one on the road.

"I think the Apache are gone," he called to his outriders when they drew within a hundred yards of the wagons. "Anyone see anything moving?"

"Just those damned vultures circling over our heads," the man who reminded Longarm of a grizzly bear and whose name was Moses replied.

When Longarm reached the wagons, he dismounted and tied his borrowed horse to a wheel. There wasn't a sound except the buzzing of horseflies, which had already found the three bodies and were intent on getting their fill of the bodily juices before the vultures appeared.

Longarm shoed the flies away, and quickly inspected each of the three dead mule skinners. They'd all been shot multiple times in the head and upper torso, and he knew that they must have died instantly. He saw no evidence that any of the three had even been given enough of a warning to return fire against their ambushers.

"All dead!" Longarm called out. "Anyone see anything moving out there?"

"The Apache headed west," one of the men said. "I don't know how many, but there were a bunch."

Longarm remounted and rode out to inspect the tracks. He remained in his saddle and tried to read the tracks, finally announcing, "I think there were at least five Apache, although it's hard to tell because they were driving all those mules. Anyone here read it any different?"

"I do," Moses said in his deep, rumbling voice. "I don't think the ambushers were Apache."

Longarm raised his eyebrows in question. "Why not?"

"Because the saddle horses were shod. Also, one of the ambushers dismounted over there and took a piss; he was wearing boots, not moccasins."

"Let me see his footprints."

Moses reined his horse through the heavy brush, and then dismounted to kneel by a faint set of footprints, still clear because the man had actually tromped in his own urine. "Yep, he wore boots. No mistake about it."

"You're right," Longarm agreed.

Moses straightened. "Apache don't even have any use for horses, preferring to move on foot. And I never knew one yet that bothered to shoe a horse."

"They might have stolen shod horses," Longarm said, "but they wouldn't be caught dead wearing high-heeled cowboy boots."

"That's the way I see it too," Moses told him. "My guess is that Travis Oates just jumped to the wrong conclusion and his men were killed by *outlaws*, not Indians."

Longarm twisted around in his saddle. "And I think I know who might be behind this attack."

"Yeah?"

"A bunch of killers from West Virginia."

Moses frowned. "Now why would anyone come that far just to steal some mules?"

"They came looking for gold," Longarm said. "They have a treasure map, and there's supposed to be a cache

141

of gold hidden here by a dying Confederate cavalryman named 'Honest' Willard Bugabee."

Moses couldn't help but smile. "That's a new one on me, and I've been in this country for six years. Now, I ain't saying there isn't buried treasure in these parts, and I have been lookin' for it like most everyone else when I can, but I never heard of 'Honest' Willard Bugabee, and that's a name a fella wouldn't easily forget."

"I believe the ambushers are the Haskill men. Their leader is named Jude and he's bad to the bone."

"How come you know all about these Haskills?" another man asked, joining them.

"It's a long, complicated story," Longarm replied. "But I ought to tell you that I'm a deputy United States marshal out of Denver, Colorado."

Moses and the other volunteers were shocked, and the big man said, "You ain't lookin' to arrest any of us, are you, Marshal?"

"No," Longarm assured them. "And whatever you did or might have done to break the law in the past is your own business. I mean to track down and either arrest or kill the Haskill men. How would all three of you like to be deputized?"

Moses shook his head. "Not me. I ain't afraid of a fight, but I'm no fool. Like I told you, there were at least five whites that ambushed that supply train."

Longarm reached into his pocket and pulled out his wallet. He counted his money, and there was thirty dollars in cash. "Here's ten dollars for any man who is willing to be deputized. I'm expecting more money from the federal government when I return to Tucson."

Moses pulled on his thick black beard. "These five men who ambushed the freight wagons have horses and saddles," he said. "Guns and watches and maybe some cash on 'em. What happens to all that booty if we catch 'em?"

"I'd split it among whoever helps me either capture or kill the Haskills. It could add up to a hell of a lot for each of you men. The mules, though, and anything the killers stripped from the bodies, go back to Oates and the families of the men that were ambushed."

Longarm studied the three and judged them to be tough, capable fighters. "What do you say, Moses? How about it, men? You might each get as much as a hundred dollars."

"And we might get killed."

Moses grunted. "If you don't join us, Henry, then that means more money for me. What about you, Otis?"

"I'm in," Otis said. "I knew those three dead freighters, and they were good men. Two of 'em have wives and kids down in Tucson. I'd like to see that whoever killed 'em gets caught and hanged. And besides that, I'm dead broke."

"All right," Henry said, "I'm with you. But I sure never thought I'd be a United States deputy."

Longarm had a paper and pencil. He gave Moses Billy Vail's name and where the man could be reached by telegraph so that, if he were killed by the Haskill men, these three would be able to collect some payment for their service to the government.

"I hereby deputize all three of you men. If I am killed, you can file for payment with the federal government in Denver, Colorado."

Moses nodded, folded the scrap of paper in his pocket, and stared out across the desert. "We ain't got any water, so we're going to have to go back and get some before we light out after that bunch."

Longarm agreed. "Let's pack the bodies up on our horses and lead them back to the saloon. It'll be a long, hot walk, but we've no choice because we can't leave those poor devils here for the vultures."

Moses looked up at the birds, and his lips drew back

in a snarl. The vultures were higher now, but still circling and hopeful. The big man raised his rifle, but Longarm pushed it down. "The ambushers might only be a few miles away. We don't want to warn them."

"Right," Moses grunted, "but I sure do hate those black birds of death."

Longarm understood. There was something about vultures that a man just naturally hated. Maybe, he thought, because they reminded him of how he might wind up with them picking the meat off his bones.

Chapter 13

Jude Haskill figured that things could not have gone better the last few days despite the killing twenty-four-hour-a-day heat. But it was worth the suffering considering that he and his brothers had stolen a herd of damn fine mules, had plenty of water and a map that was about to lead them to buried gold right here in the vicinity of Picacho Peak, Arizona.

"Hell," Jude said after killing the freighters, "even if we don't find Uncle Willard's hidden gold, we'll still be well off with all these extra weapons and four teams of big mules."

"We should have taken the freight wagons and grain too," Drew Haskill said. "We'd have gotten a lot of money for 'em up either in Phoenix or down in Tucson."

Jude glared at his brother; the one that people said most resembled him in appearance and personality. But not, Jude thought, in brains, because Drew never thought anything out to its final conclusion. Rather, he acted on impulse, and then always seemed surprised by the bad consequences.

"Drew," Jude said, "I explained several times why we couldn't take the wagons and that grain to either Tucson or Phoenix. It's because we'd have to say how we got 'em, and that would get us into a passel of trouble."

"No trouble we can't handle," Drew said stubbornly. "There are five us, and I figure we could take care of ourselves against any town marshal."

But Jude wasn't buying that argument. "I've heard that both towns are big, and they probably have a whole bunch of deputies. Use your head! We're about to find a fortune in gold out here, and we don't need to take any stupid risks."

"He's right," Abel Haskill grunted, picking his teeth with a cactus spine. "We're gonna be rich enough without having to take on a whole bunch of big-town lawmen."

The youngest members of the family, Micah and Peter, nodded in solemn agreement. They were identical twins and nineteen years old. Shorter, broader, even more muscular than their older brethren, and they were mysterious and prone to fits of terrible anger. Micah and Peter rarely said a word except to each other. Anyone who crossed one of the twins would have to take on the other, so most members of the Haskill family, Jude included, tended to leave them alone. No one had ever heard the twins have a disagreement, or even, for that matter, have opposing ideas. Micah and Peter not only looked alike, they acted and thought alike and could read each other's minds.

Jude secretly feared his youngest brothers, but they were tough, merciless fighters, unfailingly loyal and very good with their weapons.

"Let's see here now," Jude mused aloud as he sat down in the shade of a tall, five-armed saguaro cactus and unfolded the treasure map drawn by Honest Willard and stolen from his nieces, the Bugabee sisters. Piecing the two halves together, Jude laid them carefully on the ground and stared at the map for a long time, although he had already memorized its every detail.

Lifting his eyes toward Picacho Peak, he pronounced,

146

"Boys, we are on the west side of the peak, and the gold can't be more than a half mile away from where we are standing."

"That might be true," Abel said, "but there's a lot of rock, sand, and cactus out here, and it's way too hot to spend much time poking around in the sun. We've got to narrow our search down."

"I know," Jude muttered, his eyes taking in every detail of the barren landscape surrounding them. "The way I read this map, we should find an arroyo just up ahead that drains water dumped by thunderstorms off this side of the peak. If we can find the arroyo, we follow it back out this way a quarter mile and look for a large white boulder."

"There are boulders all over this godforsaken desert," Drew said. "And we don't know what size it's supposed to be."

"That's right," Jude admitted, "but the map says that the boulder we want to find is almost square and there's a scoop or rain catch basin on top filled with three round red pebbles. If we find those pebbles, then we're within ten feet of where the gold is hidden in one of the boulder's crevasses."

Jude looked up at the peak, which was less than a half mile away, and then made what he knew would be a contentious decision. "Abel," he said, "you need to stay here with the mules and make sure they don't run off. The rest of us can spread out and ride about ten feet apart straight for the peak. One of us ought to come upon the arroyo."

"What if there are a lot of arroyos?" Drew challenged.

Jude folded up the map and carefully placed it in his shirt pocket. "Then we track each one until we find the square boulder. Remember, it's white with a water catch basin on top holding three red pebbles."

The sun was blazing down from overhead, but they were all sweating almost as much from excitement as heat. Abel wasn't happy to be left behind with the mules.

147

"I don't see why it's me that has to stay with these damned mules."

"One of us has to," Jude said. "And you're the best of us with animals. Don't worry, we'll bring the gold right back here and split it up into even shares."

"I'd still rather go looking for it than stay behind," Abel groused. "You're always telling people what to do, Jude. Why don't *you* stay here with the damned mules? My eyes are as sharp as yours."

"Because I'm not going to!" Jude told the disgruntled man. "Stop your damned whining and do what I say. We'll find the gold and come right back. I can't believe you'd think we might run off and leave you with all those mules worth so much money."

"You might if my share of the gold was worth more than the mules," Abel said bluntly.

Jude felt an urge to stomp Abel, but it was too hot and the gold fever was too strong upon him to waste the time, so he said, "You better watch over those mules and don't let them get away. They're worth a lot of money, and I'll take it out of your stubborn hide if you lose even one."

Jude mounted his horse. Drew, Micah, and Peter did the same. "All right, boys," Jude said. "Keep your eyes open for the arroyo or the white boulder. The sooner we find the gold, the sooner we get out of this hellish desert."

They started riding through the hot, dry creosote brush and cactus. The going was slow and difficult because the terrain was so rough and clogged. Picacho Peak seemed to loom almost directly overhead and radiate a black, evil heat. They were nearly to its base when Drew shouted, "I see it! I see the arroyo and the white boulder. It's gotta be the right one because it's almost square!"

Jude reined his horse to the left and went crashing through the rocks and brush, as did the twins. When they all came together at the base of the large white rock resting in a wide arroyo, they knew that it was the one in their treasure map.

"Micah," Jude said, "you and your brother hold our horses while Drew and I climb up on top and make sure that this one has a stone basin with three red pebbles."

The twins said nothing as they took charge of the sweaty saddle horses. Drew and Jude easily scrambled up the east side of the white boulder, which was about the size and shape of a Concord stagecoach.

Drew was younger and quicker than Jude, and got to the stone basin first. "They're here!" he shouted, snatching up three red pebbles. "I found 'em! We got the right boulder."

Jude grinned, his eyes jumping from point to point across the top of the boulder like a water bug does across a still pond. Both men quickly realized that the huge boulder they were perched upon was cracked in a dozen places. Some of the cracks were deep and others were just on the surface.

"Willard wouldn't have dropped the gold in one of the deeper cracks," Jude reasoned aloud. "Hell, if he had, there is no way that we could even reach it."

"Then we need to examine all the shallow ones," Drew said, pulling out his bowie knife and kneeling down to start scraping into a crack partially filled with dried mud and coarse sand. "This could take some time. Didn't the damned map say anything about *which* crack hid the gold?"

"No," Jude growled, removing his hat and wiping his head and face with a dirty bandanna. His face was flushed and his shirt was soaked with salty sweat. When he looked at Picacho Peak looming overhead, he felt as if he were being watched by a black witch with evil intentions. Heat waves radiated off the dark rocks and the desert. A vulture circled in the sky, and a scorpion scuttled across a rock and disappeared into one of the deeper cracks.

"Damn," Jude muttered, feeling the sweat run fast down his spine and his tongue bulge in his mouth. "Standing on the top of this white rock is like standing in a frying pan. It must be a hundred and fifty degrees up here, and not a breath of air to cool a man down."

Drew nodded, mopping his own face as he dug furiously at the cracks in the rocks. "Do you think the gold could be in more than one of these crevices?"

"I hope not."

"Me too," Drew said, panting from his exertions and the punishment of the sun. "Maybe we should give this up and wait until the sun goes down. Otherwise, we might get our brains fried. I heard that a man tetched by the sun can go crazy."

Jude could see the sense in that, but after all this time and given the long road they'd traveled all the way from West Virginia, he just couldn't stop scraping and digging at the rock.

"Drew, let's give it an hour," he said. "Why don't you go down and get us a couple of canteens of water?"

"Not me," Drew said. "If you're that thirsty, then you get the water."

Neither of them trusted the other, and both knew it. If part of the treasure was found, one might hide it in his boot top or his pants pocket and never say a word.

"We'll both get the canteens when we have to," Jude grunted, his own bowie knife frantically gouging and probing at cracks. The scratching of hard steel against hard rock was loud and annoying, and it pained Jude to think of what he was doing to his best knife.

"You find anything up there yet?" Micah called from down where he and his twin brother held their horses and were crouched in the scant shade of the white boulder.

"Not yet," Jude yelled. "Toss us up a full canteen of water and take the others off the saddles and put 'em beside you in the shade where they'll stay cooler."

A canteen sailed up to the top, and almost dropped down one of the biggest cracks, where it would have been forever lost. Jude pounced on it and uncapped the neck. He and Drew were so parched and overheated that they emptied it in seconds; then they dropped the empty canteen and went back to work. Jude chose a two-foot-wide crack that looked promising, but that was clogged with coarse sand and a few small but vicious cholla cactus that probably survived off the rare rains that collected and then seeped down through the top of the boulder. He was in such a hurry to dig the offending cactus out that he wound up brushing against the cholla and getting the back of his right hand pincushioned in fifty places.

"Ouch!" he cried, his knife clattering on the rock as he waved his hand and swore vehemently. "Dammit!"

The barbs stung worse than hornets, and Jude gritted his teeth to keep from crying out again as he clenched his damaged hand by the wrist as if he could throttle back the intense pain. "Shit, they hurt!"

Drew glanced over, sweat pouring off his red face. "Jude, that was pretty stupid. Better use your left hand to dig."

There were times when Jude was capable of killing one of his brothers, and this was such a time. His left hand almost snaked across his waist toward his gun, but he managed to get his anger under control, and instead picked up his bowie knife, whose blade was already dull and badly nicked by the hard, white rock.

He began to dig again, slower now, and much more carefully, as he tried to slide his blade under the cholla and slice away their hard, tenacious roots. But even with great care, he still managed to get his left hand impaled by several of the vicious barbs. Jude glared at both his injured hands, fought down the pain, and kept digging. He could extract the cactus spines later . . . right now he either had to find the gold, or get off this rock before his brain fried like eggs in a skillet.

"I found something!" Drew cried, his blade slashing at the sand and dirt that had filled one of the wider cracks. "It's . . . it's gold!"

Jude dropped his knife and scuttled over to his brother. "Get it out!"

"I'm trying."

"Here," Jude said, trying to tear the knife from his younger brother's hand. "I'll do it."

"No."

A moment later, Drew shoved his fist down into the crack and plucked at a stiff old buckskin bag stuffed with gold nuggets. In a final yank, the bag tore open, and nuggets spilled from the rotting leather and rolled into the catch basin beside the three red pebbles.

Both men rocked back on their heels and stared at the nuggets. Finally, Jude whispered reverently, "Why, Drew, I swear there must be ten pounds of pure gold."

"More like fifteen, I'd say." Drew picked up an especially large nugget, polished it against the stubble of his sweaty cheek, and then put it between his back teeth and bit down hard.

"It's gold, all right," he said, grinning from ear to ear as he studied his tooth marks. "Gawdammit, we're finally rich!"

The two men jumped up and started screaming and shouting. Down below, the twins knew what was going on, but kept hold of the four saddle horses. And a quarter mile away, Abel Haskill swore in anger because he could not be there to see the gold that would soon make him and his brothers the richest men in his part of dirt-poor West Virginia.

"We did it!" Drew screamed, dancing and shouting atop the white boulder. "Boys, we're rich!"

"Look," Jude said, stooping low. "There was an old piece of paper inside that buckskin bag."

"Does it say anything?"

Jude unfolded the parchment, and saw that the writing had almost been completely spoiled by rain, but that the wording was still faint and legible. "Maybe it says there is more gold buried close by."

"Can you read it, Jude?"

He stared, and then wiped the perspiration that burned his eyes. "It says . . . it says that this gold is . . . is to be used to help the poor."

"That's it?" Drew asked.

"It says more that I can't read. Words have been lost and ruined. But I can read that much and there's a name . . . Willard Bugabee."

Drew howled, closed his eyes, and turned his face to the sky. "Well, old 'Honest' Willard, don't you worry, hoss! We *are* poor and we'll put this gold to damn good use starting with whores and whiskey! So rest easy, wherever you may be!"

Jude thought that the letter and his brother's remark were hilarious, and did a little dance before he yanked his six-gun from his holster and emptied it. Then they were all laughing and hooting and firing their guns at the sky and at brooding Picacho Peak.

The sound of the Haskill men's wild gunfire echoed off the landmark mountain, and then rolled into the desert stage station where Longarm his new deputies were digging graves and fixing to even the deadly score.

Chapter 14

When Longarm and the men he'd deputized heard the sound of distant gunshots coming from the other side of Picacho Peak, they stopped digging and headed for their weapons and horses.

"Each of us should carry at least three canteens," Longarm told Moses and the other two who were riding with him. "And make sure that your weapons are in good working order."

"That gunfire might not have come from the ambushers," Moses said.

"That's right," Longarm replied. "It could be a fight between prospectors and a band of raiding Apache. On the other hand, it sounded like a celebration, and there's only one explanation for that in this country . . . finding gold."

Longarm borrowed a horse, and just before they left the saloon and stage station, Ruby hurried over with a rifle in her hand. "I'm coming with you."

"No."

"Boris was my cousin and you know what they did to him and to Nola," she said. "So don't try to stop me because, the minute you ride off, I'll be following along right behind you men."

Longarm could see that it was useless to argue. And far too hot. "All right, Ruby, you win. Just make sure that you pack enough water for yourself and whoever's horse you're borrowing."

"I want to be deputized like the others."

"What?"

"You heard me."

"But you're a woman!"

"So?"

"Nobody ever heard of a woman deputy," Longarm argued, aware that his other newly deputized men were listening with more than a casual interest.

"Then I'll be the first and maybe the last," Ruby pronounced. "If I make it back to Denver, I want to be able to tell Nola that I was a United States deputy. It'll also make for lively conversation back in West Virginia. And besides that, I expect to be paid just as much as these three other jaspers."

There was some grumbling from Moses and the other two deputies, but Longarm squelched it when he said, "If you're willing to fight and maybe get killed, then you'll earn deputy's pay. If I get killed, put your claim in with Billy Vail back in Denver."

Ruby looked pleased. "Do you have any deputy badges we can wear?"

"No."

"Damn." Ruby looked sorely disappointed. "I sure would have liked to wear a badge just like a real Western lawman."

Longarm reached into his shirt pocket and gave her his own badge. "Wear this one if it makes you feel any braver. But I want it returned when the fight is over."

"Thanks, Custis!" Ruby winked. "If you keep being so nice to me, you'll be well rewarded."

Despite the heat and the grim circumstances they faced, all three of Longarm's deputies laughed.

Longarm didn't offer even a hint of a smile, partly because his lips would have cracked. "Let's ride out and find those Haskill ambushers," he said. "And although I'll give them the chance to surrender, they'll most likely fight to the death."

"Five against five now," Moses said, "if we count the little woman."

"Oh, you can count on me doing my part," Ruby told the big man. "Just keep your lumbering carcass down low when the Haskills open fire because every one of them backwoods boys is a true marksman."

The owner of the saloon came rushing outside and gave Longarm three sticks of dynamite. "These just might come in handy," he said, shoving them into Longarm's hands. "I used dynamite to blow a hole in the rock for a cellar saloon. The cellar comes in handy if the Apache attack and torch the place. It's also where I can keep my beer cool."

Longarm wasn't sure that he wanted dynamite, but he thanked the man and stuffed the dynamite into his saddlebags. Next, he tied his canteens down and mounted the borrowed horse, which was a tall strawberry roan with a head shaped like a big wooden shipping trunk. When he touched his heels to the high-spirited roan, it shot forward so fast that it almost dumped Longarm over the back of his saddle.

They rode at a trot with the sun hotter than Longarm could ever remember. Everything in sight seemed to be suffering, even the cactus, rocks, and creosote brush. Longarm guessed it could not be more than a few miles around Picacho Peak, so that meant that the shooting couldn't have originated from far away.

They were riding around the north side of the peak and

into the west, so the late afternoon sun, unfortunately, was shining directly into their faces. Longarm's horse stepped into a hole and a rattlesnake gave its ominous warning. The roan jumped, and just missed being struck by the poisonous viper.

Moses drew his revolver, but Longarm hissed, "No!"

"Sorry," the big man said. "It's a natural reaction."

"Save killing for the Haskill brothers," Longarm told him. "Ruby?"

"Yeah?"

"You put old Willard's map to memory. Do you think we're getting close to where the gold was to be found?"

"I do. Uncle Willard's map showed that the gold was hidden on the west side of the peak on top of a flat white boulder. I don't see the boulder, but it would likely be just up ahead. Custis, do you think that the Haskill men have already found that gold?"

"I expect so," Longarm replied. "Or else why would they shoot off their guns?"

"Maybe they're being attacked by the Apache."

"Maybe," Longarm told her, "but I doubt it. A gun battle would have lasted longer."

"Yeah," Ruby said, mopping sweat from her face. "I expect it would have."

Longarm raised his hand and whispered, "All right. Everyone dismount and we'll go ahead on foot. Quiet now, and no one shoots until I've given the order."

There was some grumbling because Moses and the others were worried about disturbing another rattlesnake. But on the other hand, walking did offer far more concealment than riding.

"Listen!" Ruby hissed a short time later. "I think I hear voices."

They all stopped and listened. "You're right," Moses grunted. "I kin hear 'em too."

"It's them," Longarm said. "I recognize Jude's voice."

Longarm was about to say something else when he heard two quick gunshots.

"What the hell?" Moses asked, looking to Longarm for an explanation.

"I don't know," he replied.

"It's Jude," Ruby said. "I'd bet my last pair of britches that he shot at least two of his brothers so he could receive a bigger share of the gold that they just found."

Longarm asked, "I know he's evil and ruthless, but would he really do that?"

"You bet he would," Ruby said without a moment's hesitation. "Jude would slit his own mother's throat for a dollar and change."

"Then the odds have just shifted in our favor," Longarm told his deputies. "And from the sound of the gunshots, I'd say that the Haskill men are not more than a quarter mile up ahead."

"And damn near at the base of the peak," Moses said as the last dying echoes fled across the desert floor. "Why don't we just mount up and charge 'em? I hate waitin', and I'd like to get this fight over quick."

"That would be a bad mistake," Longarm told the big man. "Being crack shots, they'd shoot you off your horse before you got a chance to return their fire."

"He's right," Ruby said. "They'd be hunched down in the rocks and brush and they'd drill all five of us."

"Then what are we going to do?" Moses demanded. "It's too hot to be waiting around out here under this sun."

"We'll tie up our horses behind these rocks and circle them on foot," Longarm decided. "Moses, you and your friends circle around to the north and come in behind them on the east side so they can't run off. Ruby, you and I will give them fifteen minutes and then move in from this side. If all goes well, we'll have the Haskill brothers caught in a crossfire and they will either surrender or die."

"Like I said before," Ruby told him, "Jude will never

surrender. And neither will his brothers, one of them probably being Drew. Jude and Drew are thicker'n than flies on fresh pig shit."

"You hear that, boys?" Longarm asked as his newly appointed deputies got ready to go into a flanking maneuver. "Two marksmen are up ahead, maybe even more. So be careful and keep your heads *low*."

Moses nodded, and the others tied their horses where they couldn't be seen and then followed him into the brush, each carrying a full canteen. It was going to be hot, dangerous work, but Longarm figured the fight would be fast and furious. It wouldn't last more than a few minutes, and he hoped that when it ended, Jude and every other Haskill man would either be dead or wounded.

Longarm pulled out his watch and noted that the time was four-fifteen. He clutched the Ingersoll tightly and said to Ruby, "We'll give them until four-thirty and then we'll move."

Longarm and Ruby found a thin strip of shade in the shadow of a saguaro and waited, sipping water from their canteens and watching for scorpions. Longarm frequently consulted his pocket watch, and just when it was about time to move, he heard four rifle shots that blended into one burst of rolling thunder.

"What happened!" Ruby cried.

"I don't know. Let's move!"

Longarm ran ahead, but being tall, he had to stoop low, and the ground was so rough that most of the time he was looking at his next step rather than ahead toward where the rifles had fired. Ruby was right on his heels, and doing a lot better at making her way soundlessly through the rocks and brush.

A rifle boomed, and Longarm's flat-brimmed Stetson went sailing across the brush. He struck the ground and landed on a tarantula that had been trying to get out of his way. The hairy spider jumped straight up into his face, and Longarm's heart skipped a beat. But the insect bounced off his cheek, then disappeared into the brush.

More rifle shots clipped leaves and branches over their heads, and then they both heard the sound of racing hooves.

"Something went wrong," Longarm said as he eased himself up on his knees and peered over the sage. "Moses!"

Longarm thought he heard a groan, but he couldn't be sure. "Ruby, I'm afraid that my new deputies have all been shot. We'd better get help to them quick."

They started running through the brush, tripping over deadfall and rocks and shouting for Moses and his friends to answer.

Ruby shouted, "There they are!"

Longarm spotted the big man and his two companions lying in a dishlike depression. Two of the deputies were flat on their backs, faces absent of expression, eyes staring directly into the sun. Moses was the only one that was moving, and it was clear that he was in bad shape.

"What happened?" Longarm asked when he reached the big man's side.

Moses was pale and gripping his left arm, but the blood was still leaking between his thick fingers. "The bastards were laying for us up on that big white boulder. They had the high ground and drilled us before we could find cover."

"How many?"

"Two or three. I don't know. They didn't miss. We were caught out in the open and it was like shooting fish in a rain barrel." Moses glanced over at his two dead friends and swore in helpless frustration.

When Ruby tore a strip of cloth from her shirt and wrapped it around the wounded man's arm, Moses grabbed Longarm and said, "We gotta kill them ambushing bastards!"

161

"You're in no shape to fight."

"I can ride a horse," Moses insisted. "I'm coming with you, and we better go *now*."

Longarm could see a dust trail, and he knew that Jude and his brothers were moving fast. He looked at Ruby and said, "I don't suppose there's much point in asking you to stay here."

"Don't waste your breath."

"All right then, let's hurry back to the horses and see if we can catch Jude before he gets away free." Longarm paused for a moment. "Moses, I'm sorry this happened to you and your friends."

"Wasn't your fault. The Haskills were marksmen, all right. Not a wasted shot. The put two bullets in Otis, one in Henry, and the last one clipped me in the arm. If I hadn't been able to roll into this low spot, I'd also be knockin' on St. Peter's door. Let's git 'em, Marshal!"

"We'll do our best," Longarm promised.

When they reached their horses and mounted up, they rode hard after the thin dust cloud moving southwest. Longarm wondered where the stolen mules were being kept, and he figured there had to be one, maybe two other Haskill men in charge of the valuable mules.

Four to two. Maybe five to our two, he thought as they galloped through the sage not even thinking about Honest Willard's old treasure map or its promise of gold. So far, all they had found was heat, dust, and death.

Chapter 15

When Jude and Drew galloped up to the place where Micah and Peter were holding the mules, the twins were full of questions. Mostly, they wanted to know if old man Willard Bugabee's treasure map had lead to the long-anticipated gold discovery.

"We went right to where the map said the gold was supposed to be hidden, but there wasn't a damn thing to be found," Jude lied. "We located the big white rock and there were even three red pebbles in a basin on top, but no gold. Ain't that right, Drew?"

"That's right. The map was a fake, but at least we have all these mules to sell down in Tucson."

Peter and Micah exchanged looks, but said nothing.

"Boys," Jude said, "we need to mount up and get moving."

Micah was staring at Jude and Drew's saddlebags, which appeared to be a whole lot fuller than they had been earlier that day. Micah said, "We heard the shots. What happened to Abel?"

Jude twisted around in his saddle toward Picacho Peak. "Abel is dead. He was shot by three men who were sneaking up on us. As soon as they got Abel, we drilled all three of the bastards. But there might be more men coming. That's why we have to stop jawin' and get on the move."

"Who were they?" Micah demanded.

"What does it matter?" Jude answered.

The twins stiffened, and it was Peter who said, "It matters that we know what happened just now and what we're up against."

"I told you that," Jude said. "There were three men, but we killed them after they shot Abel."

Micah removed his hat and squinted up at his oldest brother. "Jude, you and Drew should have brought Abel's body along with you so we could have at least given him a decent burial."

"No time for that," Jude said, studying the restless and heat-stressed mules. "We need to get our stock to water."

Drew Haskill uncorked his canteen and drained it dry. "Jude is right. We're low on water and we need to get moving just in case there are others tracking us and these mules from those wagons we left on the road."

"But maybe you found the wrong rock," Peter agued. "Maybe the map is still right and there's a treasure in gold waiting to be found within a rock's throw of us."

"Honest Willard's map was a fake!" Jude shouted, pulling the map out of his shirt pocket and shredding it before tossing the pieces up into the hot air. "Forget the damned map! We've got all these mules to sell."

Micah looked at his brother, and silent but strong unspoken thoughts passed between them that something was fishy . . . something wasn't right.

Peter's hand came to rest on the butt of his gun, and Micah's hand did the same. "Jude, we intend to collect Abel's body and give him a decent burial."

"At the risk of your lives?" Jude demanded.

"Yep," Micah said. "Peter and I couldn't face our kinfolk back home if we left Abel to feed the vultures."

"Look," Jude said, trying hard to keep his composure. "There's no telling how many more men might be coming after us. One of them could even be Custis Long."

"Then we'll kill him the same as we killed Cousin Boris," Peter said matter-of-factly.

"Custis doesn't matter anymore," Drew argued. "We came here because of their uncle's treasure map, but it was a fool's chase. All of us are disappointed that Willard's map was a fake, but at least we have these mules and some extra guns and rifles to sell. Boys, we'll go home far richer than we left. So listen to Jude and let's quit arguing and ride."

Micah stiffened. "Like we told you, we can't leave Abel's body to the vultures."

Jude looked over at Drew. "Did you hear that?"

"I did," Drew said.

Jude raised his hand and pointed off toward where Abel had died. "Then I guess we'd better dig a grave for Abel."

The twins relaxed. Micah said, "It's the decent and honorable thing to do. I'm glad that you see it our way, Jude."

"Oh," he replied, drawing his six-gun and leveling it at Micah, "I sure do."

"What the hell are you doing!" Micah demanded as Drew also pulled his gun and pointed it at the twins.

"We're going to let you boys stay here and give poor Abel a proper funeral while we move along to Tucson."

"You can't leave us out here! For Gawd sakes, we're your brothers!"

"Yeah," Jude said, "but you've always been a contrary pair of sonofabitches and I never much liked either one of you. Drew, disarm 'em."

"You gonna just shoot us?" Peter asked, his face turning pale.

"No," Jude said, "I'm going to let you live to bury Abel. I'm even going to give you your weapons back. I'll put 'em on the same white rock that was on the map and hope you find them."

Micah blanched. "You ain't really leaving us out here in this desert, are you, Jude?"

"I am," he replied. "Your weapons and a full canteen will be waiting for you on the white rock with three red pebbles. It's not more than a quarter mile away and you shouldn't have any trouble finding it. As for your horses and the mules, well, we'll be taking them."

"You're leaving us on foot!" Peter shouted. "If you do that, why don't you just put a bullet in our heads?"

"Because I think that we're being followed by Marshal Custis Long and I want you boys to show him and whoever is with our cousin what fine marksmen you both are."

Micah was shaking with fury as Drew disarmed him and his brother. "You're by far the worst of us," he said. "You're the one that talked us all into coming out West to find gold. You're the one that tortured Boris. We should never have trusted you."

"That's right," Jude said with a smile. "And I'm sorry to leave you in this fix. If you somehow manage to kill Custis Long and his friends, then maybe you can catch up with me and Drew and we'll all make up and be brothers again."

But Peter was shaking his head. "You do this to us . . . your own brother . . . we ain't never gonna forgive or forget."

"Yeah," Jude said, "I expect not. But I'll worry about that some other day . . . if you boys survive Custis and this desert."

Micah's voice shook with fury. "You're a hound from hell and by Gawd we'll hunt you both down!"

"I don't think so," Jude said, firing once and blowing Micah's knee apart.

Micah screamed, and when his brother lunged at Jude, Drew cracked him across the skull with the barrel of

166

his pistol. Peter fell hard, and both men were writhing in pain when their older brothers rode off driving the extra horses and the stolen mules.

Drew said, "I didn't think you'd do it."

"Didn't want to," Jude said. "We could have used them, but they were so damned stubborn about burying Abel that I just got tired of listening to their yap."

"If they make it, we'll be looking over our backs all the way to West Virginia. You know the twins won't rest until they kill us or we kill them."

"Yeah," Jude said, "I know. But in the first place, I expect Custis to kill the both of them. And in the second place, I'm not going back to West Virginia."

"You ain't?"

"Nope," Jude said. "I'm taking my half of the gold and heading for California."

"But what about the family?"

"What family?"

Drew was silent for a few minutes as they rode along, then said, "Maybe I'll go to California with you."

"Might be a good idea," Jude offered, glancing up at the vultures that were circling overhead.

"The only thing is, I'll be wondering if you're thinking of killing me and keeping all the gold for yourself."

Jude forced a smile. "Now brother, why would I do a thing like that?"

"Because you're greedy, same as me."

"Greedy, but not dumb. We need each other to get these mules down to Tucson. Then we got to watch each other's backs from now on. Besides, thanks to the gold nuggets in our saddlebags and all these mules, we're *both* rich."

Drew studied his brother not believing a word of it. "Yeah, but a man like you can never be rich enough."

"Then we'll just have to see what happens," Jude said with a cold smile. "All I know for sure is that, by tomorrow night, we'll be celebrating in Tucson."

They laughed, but each man knew that he could not trust the other as they pushed the thirsty mules across the blistering Sonoran Desert.

An hour after sundown and still twenty brutal miles northwest of Tucson, Jude and Drew got lucky and came upon a pair of prospectors camped beside a spring with their burros. The prospectors were in their forties and had been together a long time, tough men who had poked around together in the deserts of Arizona for many years. They were also wary of strangers and not prone to being hospitable.

"Hold up there and state your names and your business!" the bigger one, named Elmer, yelled as he brandished his ancient black-powder rifle.

"We need water!" Jude croaked, his throat so parched that when he swallowed, it felt like he had a mouthful of sand.

"How many of them are you?" the prospector demanded, eyes squinted as he peered into the moonlit evening at all the livestock.

"Two, but we got a bunch of mules and extra horses. We're in tough shape and need water real bad."

"Elmer, tell 'em we own this spring and charge money for water," the smaller of them, named Gus, whispered from the cover of bushes. "If they got that many mules, they got enough money to pay us well."

"Good idea.

"This is our property," Elmer called. "If you want water, you'll have to pay us two bits for every animal that drinks!"

"All right! We'll pay."

"We will?" Drew asked. "Why don't we just kill 'em. I figure there's only two old men camped here."

"We'll kill them, but not while they got rifles pointed

at us," Jude said. "We got to play this out until we got the advantage."

Gus was grinning. "What did I tell you, Elmer," he whispered. "We're gonna make us five or ten dollars tonight!"

"And just in the nick of time. We was about broke."

"Tell 'em to show their money before they let the livestock get to the spring," Gus ordered.

"Mister," Elmer yelled, his rifle held at the ready, "how many horses and mules you got to water?"

"We got thirty head," Jude called, figuring it didn't matter what number he shouted.

Gus said, "Thirty head. That means they owe us . . . uh . . . tell them it'll cost ten dollars and they ain't welcome to share our company or food."

Elmer moved into the firelight. "Stranger, before you let those mules near the water, you better ride up here and pay me."

"I'll do that," Jude called, motioning Drew to stay put. "We'll wait until we've got them both in our sights before we open fire," he said softly.

"Sounds good," Drew replied.

"Just be ready," Jude warned. "It's going to be sudden."

Jude rode into the camp and dismounted, eyes searching for the second prospector. "Evening," he said, trying to look friendly. "Sure am glad you got some water. My partner and I are about ready to die of thirst, and our stock ain't doing much better."

"It's a damn hot and dry desert," Elmer said, rifle still pointed at Jude. "Let's see the color of your money."

Jude had plenty of money, thanks to the generosity of the three teamsters, whose pockets he'd emptied. He counted out ten dollars. "This is kinda high-priced for water, I'd say. Now if you were selling whiskey, I wouldn't mind forking over ten dollars."

Elmer realized they had a lot of money, and that he

169

might get even more of it. "We got whiskey too."

"I'd sure like a drink of whiskey," Jude said as the tall prospector snatched ten dollars from his hands. "I'd be willing to pay plenty for it."

"Drive your mules in and keep away from our campfire," Elmer warned. "You and your partner can water your horses and yourselves all at once. Muddy water never killed a man, and we'll talk about the whiskey soon enough."

"Much obliged," Jude told the wary prospector. "Hey, Drew, you can drive in the extra horses and mules now. Let 'em drink their fill."

Jude watched as the mules and saddle horses stampeded toward a little pond where a good well emptied. He listened, hearing the sucking and slurping sounds of the animals as they filled their bellies with water.

"Your animals are real thirsty," Elmer said. "Had those mules very long?"

"Nope. We bought them in Flagstaff and are starting a freighting company down in Tucson."

"Why'd you leave the main road and come over this far to the west?" Elmer asked suspiciously.

"We got lost."

"You lost the *road*?"

"We had business out to the west of Picacho Peak," Jude said, knowing it sounded false and wishing that the other prospector would move into the light of the campfire so that Drew could get a clean shot. But the prospector was too smart for that and stayed hidden in the darkness, no doubt with a rifle aimed and ready to fire.

"Sure would like to buy some of your whiskey," Jude said as the mules and horses continued drinking their fill.

Elmer wished he could ask Gus how much to charge; Gus was better with numbers, but Elmer had to say something, so he blurted out, "It'll cost you . . . a dollar a glass."

170

Jude acted like that was a fair price. "Be worth it to me and my partner."

"I'll get the whiskey and glasses," the prospector told him as he moved back toward his campfire. "Gus?"

"Yeah, I'm still hidin' in the bushes. What's going on?"

"They're willin' to pay a dollar a glass for whiskey," Elmer said as he found their bottle and two dirty glasses. "That's two more dollars in our pockets!"

"Ain't that somethin'," Gus said, more suspicious, but getting excited by the idea of so much cash money coming their way. "Be sure and get the money before you give him any whiskey."

"I already decided that," Elmer said, injured to think that his friend and partner had so little faith in his judgment.

When Elmer returned to the campfire, the man on horseback was still waiting. He even licked his lips when he saw the whiskey and glasses, and said, "Fill 'em to the brim, mister. For a dollar, a thirsty man ought to get a *full* glass."

Elmer set this rifle down and poured one glass, which Jude drank in a few deep, shuddering gulps before croaking, "I'll have another."

"Pay up."

Jude paid the second dollar, and this time he held the glass up to the campfire and declared, "By damned, I see something floating around in this glass of whiskey. What the hell is it?"

"Flies got into our whiskey."

Jude blinked, but recovered, and even managed to sound as if that didn't matter. "At least those flies got drunk before they drowned."

"That's right," Elmer said. "You gonna drink the second glass or take it over to your friend?"

"I'll take it over to him right now," Jude said. "Where's your partner?"

"He's close," Elmer said. "Gus is shy, but he's a good shot."

Jude got the message. He rode over to find Drew and when they joined, he whispered, "The other one is hiding behind that big cactus over yonder. Climb off your horse and sneak up behind him."

"I'll do it," Drew promised.

"Here's a glass of whiskey."

Drew emptied the glass, and heard his older brother began to giggle, causing Drew to ask, "What's so damned funny?"

"There are flies in that whiskey you just drank."

Drew coughed and spit. "Flies?"

"That's right. I drank some myself, but they didn't hurt me none as you can plainly see. Now, go shoot that fella hiding in the dark and we can stay here the rest of the night and drink up the last of that whiskey."

"I'd rather push on to Tucson," Drew said. "If Micah and Peter don't kill whoever is following us, I don't want us to be overtaken out here in this damned open desert with saddlebags full of gold and all these mules."

Jude realized that his brother was right. "Hey, mister!" he called, turning back toward the campfire.

"Yeah," Elmer replied. "What do you want now?"

"I'd like another glass of your whiskey, dead flies and all."

"You got another dollar?"

"I got *plenty* of dollars. How about another drink?"

"You get one more and then you and your outfit are movin' on," Elmer said, deciding that twelve dollars was money enough. "You can reach Tucson before sunrise, and they got plenty of whiskey in their saloons without flies and without costin' you no dollar a glass."

"We'll be moving on soon enough," Jude told the surly prospector. "Just bring me one more glass."

When the man turned his back and started toward his

campfire where he kept the bottle, Jude followed him in silence. Just then, Drew got a good shot and opened up on the second prospector, drilling Gus in the back.

"Got him!" Drew shouted.

Elmer had just bent over and retrieved the foul bottle of whiskey when he heard Drew's gunshot. The prospector dropped the bottle and lunged toward his rifle but it was already too late. Laughing hysterically, Jude shot him twice in the chest and, just for good measure, once right between the eyes.

"Well," Jude said, "now we got a pair of sorry burros to add to our collection of livestock we're fixin' to sell tomorrow."

"Yep," Drew said as he went over to the campfire and began to help himself to a pan of beans and pork. "Where's that bottle of whiskey?"

"Damned if I know," Jude said, "but you can bet we'll find and sample some more of it before we leave and swallow the last of them drunken flies."

"Wonder if they have found any gold," Drew said as he tossed more wood on the fire and began to rummage through the prospectors' belongings.

"I doubt it," Jude said, scooping the pot of beans empty with his hand.

He wiped his hand on his pants and watched as Drew finished searching for anything of value. "You'll find my ten dollars on that dead one," said Jude.

Drew emptied Elmer's pocket and shoved the money in his own pants.

"Hey," Jude protested. "That money is mine."

"Don't worry. You'll get half when we split everything even in Tucson." Drew smiled. "Hell, brother, like you said, we're rich."

"Almost," Jude muttered as he began searching for the flies and the whiskey.

Chapter 16

"Over there," Ruby called, drawing her horse up hard. "I saw something glint in the sun just ahead!"

"Where?" Longarm asked.

She pointed. "On top of that big white rock."

Longarm frowned. "Wasn't the gold supposed to be found on top of a big white rock?"

"Yes. And it even said the rock was square, like that one."

Longarm studied the rock from a distance he judged to be about four or five hundred yards. "I can't imagine why anyone in their right mind would be hiding up there waiting in ambush. The sun must be baking them alive."

"Over here!" Moses called a short distance away.

Longarm and Ruby rode over to where Moses was studying signs in the dirt. "There's plenty of blood been spilled here. And look. Whoever was shot started walking and he wasn't alone."

Moses pointed in the direction of the white rock and said, "From the amount of blood, I don't expect the man could have walked very far."

Longarm turned to Ruby. "What do you make of this?"

"I'd say that Jude shot someone but didn't finish the job."

"But who?"

Ruby shrugged her shoulders. "That's anyone's guess, but it must have been one of his own brothers."

"Moses says there are *two* walking men."

"Maybe it's the twins, Micah and Peter."

"All right," he said. "It looks like a pair of the Haskill men have been left behind to ambush us from up on that big rock."

"How the hell are we ever going to get 'em?" Moses asked, looking exhausted by the heat and his wound and plenty worried. "They got the high ground and can hold us off for hours."

Longarm agreed. "We could ride around them and keep following the mules, but I'd rather settle this first."

"Marshal, do you have a plan?" Moses asked.

Longarm knew that they could waste hours trying to flush men off that high rock. And they didn't have hours. If Jude and whoever was with him got to Tucson with time to spare, they could sell the mules, board a stagecoach or train, and be long gone from Arizona Territory by noon tomorrow, "I'll offer whoever is up there a chance to surrender," he decided.

"They won't surrender," Ruby insisted.

"I got to offer it to them anyway," Longarm said. "If they refuse, then we'll kill them and move on after the ones driving the mules."

"It'll be dark in another hour," Ruby said. "They could climb down and sneak away."

"I doubt they'll do that," Longarm said. "Especially if one of them has lost a lot of blood."

He dismounted and handed his reins to Ruby. "You and Moses stay here."

"Custis, what are you going to do?"

"Watch me," Longarm said, reaching into his saddlebags and extracting two of the three sticks of dynamite.

"Holy hog fat!" Moses exclaimed. "Are you going to do what I think you're going to do?"

"Only if they won't come down and surrender."

Longarm ducked and moved fast through the brush. Bullets from on top of the rock began coming his way, but he stayed low and gave the ambushers a poor target. However, when the rifle fire from above started getting too close, he took cover behind a fair-sized rock.

"Whoever is up there had better stop shooting and listen to me!" he yelled.

"What for!" a voice called down. "We ain't surrendering, Marshal Custis Long!"

"Do you both want to die?"

There was a long silence, and then a strained voice cried, "We ain't afraid of dying. Everyone has to die sometime."

"Who are you?"

"It's Micah and Pete. We're the ones that are gonna kill you!"

"It doesn't have to be that way," Longarm called out. "Surrender and I'll see that whichever one of you has been shot gets medical help."

"Go to hell!"

Longarm swore as he studied the dynamite in his hands. Micah and Peter were the twins, and he figured they couldn't be more than twenty years old. Too young to die needlessly.

"Last chance!" he yelled. "Don't throw your lives away for Jude and whoever else left you behind. Jude won't care if you're dead."

Longarm thought he heard some arguing on top of the high rock, so he gave the twins another few minutes.

"Come and get us, Marshal!"

"Damn," Longarm whispered. He shoved one of the sticks of dynamite into his back pocket and found a match. He lit the fuse and charged, tossing the stick of lit dynamite hard and high.

Longarm hit the ground rolling with bullets splattering around him at the same moment the dynamite went off. The explosion filled the air with rock shards, dust, and shredded vegetation, and Longarm felt the earth shake.

"Give up now!" Longarm yelled a moment later through the choking dust. "The next one lands on top and blows you both to smithereens!"

More bullets started coming Longarm's way, so he lit the second fuse. This time he was a lot closer to the rock, and made sure that the dynamite landed on top. After that, there wasn't enough left of the foolish Haskill twins to fill a teacup.

Before leaving Picacho Peak, Longarm, Ruby, and Moses found Abel buried in a shallow grave, and then they pushed on into the night following the broad tracks of the remaining Haskill men and the stolen mules. It was hard going, and they rode slowly through the night because the air was still as hot as the inside of a Dutch oven. At daybreak, they saw vultures as thick as fleas on a sick dog circling over a patch of green near some low and sun-blasted hills. Longarm was exhausted by the heat, and he could see that Ruby and Moses were hurting every bit as bad.

"There's something that's been killed just up ahead," he told Ruby. "Maybe you'd better hang back until we see what it is."

"Not a chance," she told him. "I'm a deputy just like the rest, and I'll do my job."

"Suit yourself."

They arrived at the spring and the prospectors' camp, shooing off the vultures who loudly protested their uninvited presence.

"We have to bury them," Longarm said, hating to lose the time and feeling the heat of the rising sun. "Let's get it done quick and move on to Tucson." The ground was unyielding and the digging was slow and difficult work. The vultures had started on the prospectors even before first light, and after the graves were finished, Longarm asked Ruby to say a few quick words.

"Lord," she began with her head bowed low, "receive the souls of these two poor fellas that didn't do anything to deserve being gunned down. And help us to bring their killers to a quick and final justice so they will go to hell."

"Amen," Longarm said along with Moses. "Mount up and let's ride."

It was nearly noon when Longarm, Ruby, and Moses reached Tucson, and there wasn't much of anyone on the street. But there was a train at the depot and it was blasting its whistle.

"Do you think they've already sold the mules and their horses and boarded the train?" Ruby asked.

"It's a real possibility," Longarm answered. "Especially if they know we're close on their trail."

"What are we going to do?"

Longarm expelled a deep breath and reined his tired horse toward the train depot. "We could check out the livestock buyers, but there's no time left for that now. I think we'd better hold up the train and see if Jude and whoever else is on board."

"It could get bloody and some of the passengers could get shot by accident," Ruby said.

Longarm had already come to that same conclusion. "I'll tell the conductor that we want all the passengers to get off and wait until we've done our search."

"Will he do that for you?"

Longarm nodded. "He will if you give me back my federal marshal's badge."

Ruby handed him the badge, but it was clear she wasn't happy. "It was nice wearing it for a while."

Longarm, Ruby, and Moses rode up the street to the

depot, and dismounted. It only took a few minutes to find the conductor and give the man an order to evacuate all passengers from the westbound train for California. The conductor was furious until Longarm explained that there were two or maybe even more desperate killers on board.

"All right," the conductor agreed. "But we're already five minutes behind schedule."

"This won't take long. How many passenger cars are there that we need to search?"

"Four."

Longarm described Jude. "Did you see a man fitting that description?"

"As a matter of fact I did. And one more that looked almost like him."

"I'll bet that's Drew," Ruby said. "Which car were they in?"

"The last coach is first class, and that's the car your man bought a ticket to ride in."

Longarm turned to Ruby and Moses. "You cover both sides of the train so they can't get away."

"I figure I should go with you," Moses objected.

But Longarm shook his head. "The aisles are narrow, so we'd have to go in single file, and you being there wouldn't make a difference," Longarm explained. "Just be ready to shoot if you see the Haskill men jumping off the train. We've come too far to let them escape now."

"Just be careful," Moses warned.

"I will," Longarm assured the huge man he'd deputized.

It took about ten minutes for the train to empty, and there was no sign of Jude or any of his brothers. "They know we're here," Longarm said to Moses as he checked his gun one last time. "They're waiting inside for us. Let's go."

They entered the train with guns in their hands and started with the first coach, then worked their way back to the last one, where they expected to find the Haskill men.

"If we go through that door, they're going to riddle us," Longarm said, not willing to offer himself up as Jude's next victim.

"Then what will we do?"

Longarm had an idea. "Let's get off and go see the conductor."

Twenty minutes later, the train was back on its way to California with all of its passengers except two. The first-class passengers hadn't been pleased to be reassigned to lesser cars, but when they understood the gravity of the situation, they'd stopped complaining.

"What happens now?" Ruby asked.

Longarm returned to his strawberry roan and dug into his saddlebags. He drew out the third stick of dynamite he'd been given by the saloon and station owner back at Picacho Peak, and when he raised it up to show Moses, he started grinning.

"Holy cow!" Moses exclaimed. "Are you really gonna do it to 'em?" Longarm cut the fuse short.

"Custis, would you really blow the first-class car up?" Ruby asked.

"Damn right I will," Longarm vowed. "I gave the Haskill twins two or three chances to surrender when they were up on top of that white rock. I'm giving Jude and whoever else is on this car just one chance to live or die."

He moved closer to the car and yelled, "Jude, it's Marshal Custis Long. Surrender now or get killed."

"Go to hell!"

"That's what I thought you'd say," Longarm grunted a moment before he touched a match to the stick of dynamite, hurled it right through one of the open windows, and ran like hell.

The car exploded with more fury than seemed possible. Glass, metal, and wood filled the air over Tucson, and when everything landed on the street and the railroad depot, Longarm stared at the naked frame of the first-class coach with grim satisfaction.

"Ruby, it's over."

She leaned on him. "Do you think they found our uncle's gold?"

"We can search the debris for it," Longarm suggested, his eyes just happening to spot a couple of nuggets resting near his feet. "Look," he cried, bending down to pick them up and finding them almost too hot to the touch. "I guess those Haskill brothers did find our uncle's gold after all."

Ruby began to scramble around fast, collecting nuggets faster than a starving robin could pluck worms. Longarm decided that he might as well help her out. After all, his uncle, Honest Willard Bugabee, would have approved of the way that Ruby and Nola intended to use this Arizona gold.

As it turned out, the prominent Tucson banker who had been embezzling funds had already been gunned down, but not by anyone he'd cheated. Instead, the banker had been shot by a prostitute that he'd jilted after suffering pangs of guilt over cheating on his faithful but homely wife.

Longarm sent a telegram to Billy Vail that read:

SEND ADDITIONAL FUNDS **STOP** HEAT IS TERRIBLE AND WE NEED TO GET BACK TO DENVER FOR BIG WEDDING **END**

"Do you think he'll send us enough money to get back to Denver?" Ruby asked as they left the telegraph office.

"He'll grumble, but the money will come," Longarm promised as he and Ruby headed for a hotel and a bath. "It always does."

Watch for

Longarm and Maximilian's Gold

299th novel in the exciting LONGARM series
from Jove

Coming in October!

Explore the exciting Old West with one of the men who made it wild!

AVAILABLE WHEREVER BOOKS ARE SOLD OR TO ORDER CALL:
1-800-788-6262

(Ad # B112)

**Explore the exciting Old West with one
of the men who made it wild!**

LONGARM AND THE MOUNTAIN BANDIT #267
0-515-13018-4

LONGARM AND THE LADY BANDIT #270
0-515-13057-5

LONGARM AND THE SCORPION MURDERS #271
0-515-13065-6

LONGARM AND THE GUNSHOT GANG #274
0-515-13158-X

LONGARM AND THE DENVER EXECUTIONERS #275
0-515-13184-9

LONGARM AND THE WIDOW'S SPITE #276
0-515-13171-7

*ROUND UP ALL THESE
GREAT TITLES!*

**AVAILABLE WHEREVER BOOKS ARE SOLD OR
TO ORDER CALL:**

1-800-788-6262

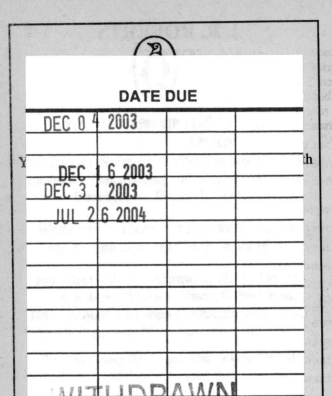

Subscribe to Penguin Group (USA) Inc. News at
http://www.penguin.com/newsletters